FELL WINTER

Book One of the Ulfr Crisis

I0673105

BADELGARD, THE COUNTRY OF THE NORTHMEN

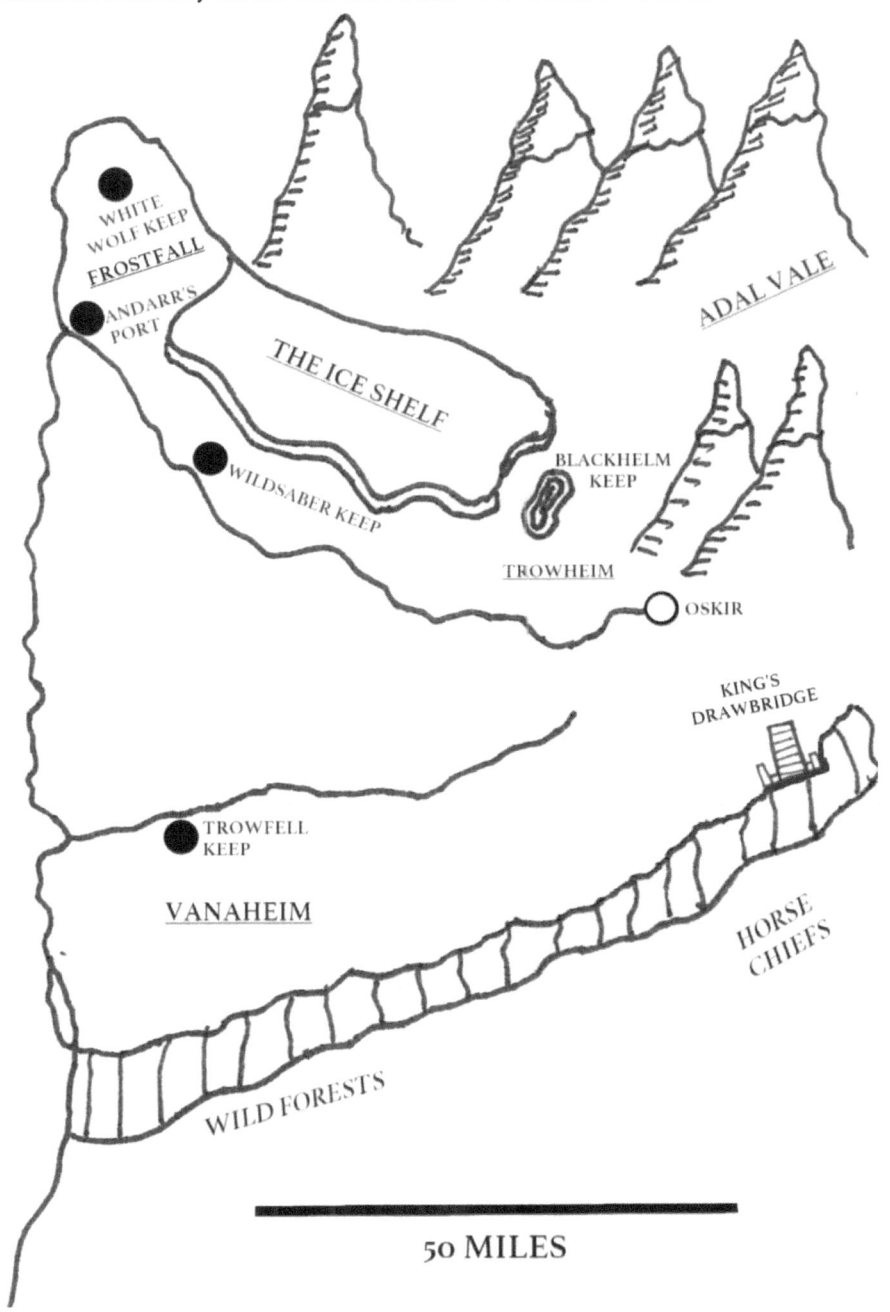

WHITE WOLF KEEP

FROSTFALL

ANDARR'S PORT

THE ICE SHELF

ADAL VALE

WILDSABER KEEP

BLACKHELM KEEP

TROWHEIM

OSKIR

KING'S DRAWBRIDGE

TROWFELL KEEP

VANAHEIM

HORSE CHIEFS

WILD FORESTS

50 MILES

Table of Contents

CHAPTER ONE

Brand, son of Gutlaff, had hair as brown as chestnuts and eyes the color of the clear blue sky. At least, that's what the women of The Lily House—Oskir's best, and only, den of iniquity—told him. They were a little biased, however; Brand paid off the lovely-eyed, smooth-skinned women with coin. His father, the straitlaced swineherd Gutlaff, had told him of the dangers of big towns and how they could corrupt a boy's morals. And corrupt Brand's morals they did.

Brand walked out, suppressing his guilt with a shrug. The visit had been a minor concession for a recent accomplishment; just an hour ago, the headmaster of the Skalds' College announced that Brand's mastery of the lute and voice was complete, and that he was worthy of servicing the court of any earl or singing the deeds of any warrior.

A stressful audition followed by three years of hard work had finally paid off. He was still lowborn, but he did not have to work in the mines, or—gods help him—take up swineherding like his father. He could sing and pluck the lute to the tune of his own destiny.

Within the college's stone walls he had learned to play the pipe, the shawm, the horn, and countless other instruments. Yet his specialty—and the musical style his teachers encouraged in him above all—was the lute and voice. Now, he could pluck his faithful instrument and sing love ballads to girls, silly songs for the wide-eyed little children, and songs of valor and brave deeds to the warriors.

Right after leaving The Lily House he ran into his best friend in the city of Oskir. Gunnar 'Blackhelm' Whoreson was his name: 'Blackhelm,' because his father was the highborn noble Magnus Blackhelm—Earl of Trowheim—and Whoreson because his mother once sold her body.

Some, including the Blackhelms, questioned that Magnus was his father. But both Brand and Gunnar were certain beyond a doubt: Gunnar's mother, right after she had taken the earl as her client, had left the life of the whorehouse for better things. She was pregnant and gave birth to Gunnar, who had the stern features of a nobleman and the famous flame-red hair of the Blackhelms.

"Did you have fun with Lucia today?" Gunnar said.

"Lucia wasn't available, unfortunately," Brand said. "She was with another man."

"So she's cheating on you… is that what you're saying?"

"Whores cannot cheat, Gunnar," Brand said, "though I admit her lack of devotion does tear on my heartstrings, as the old song goes."

"You are a singing dandy, with your head in the clouds," Gunnar said. "You've completed your schooling and now, my friend, it's time to celebrate."

"Where to?" Brand said.

"The mead hall," Gunnar said. "By midnight tonight, you won't be able to walk."

It was not Brand, but Gunnar, that did most of the drinking. The women of the mead hall—some of whom also worked at The Lily House—brought drinking-horns filled to the brim with mead.

"What now, Brand?" Gunnar said, wearing a moustache of foam. "Will you join an earl's court and go to some far-flung keep?"

"No," Brand said. "I will bond myself to a warrior and sing of his deeds…"

"And to which warrior?" Gunnar said. "To an earl's man? To an earl's bodyguard?"

"No; the earls' bodyguards only stand around all day and protect their liege." Brand thought for a while, though he knew thinking was generally a bad idea in the mead hall. "It will have to be an adventurer… someone who travels around Badelgard and has deeds worthy to sing of."

"I will travel around Badelgard, and be an adventurer, if that is what it takes to have you as my skald," Gunnar said. "I would be honored to have Brand Gutlaffson sing of my deeds."

Brand smiled. "Your axe is sturdy, Gunnar, and you wield it with skill. I will have to consider your request." He sipped some mead from his drinking horn. "But if I am to sing of your deeds, you will have to leave Oskir, Gunnar. I've seen you practice with your axe often—and win duels, at that. But I have a feeling you're content working with metal and staying inside the city walls."

"Ol' Hennard is a mean old dog. Never let me keep a single sword I made. Doesn't respect us highborn Blackhelms—guess he's too common to understand our importance," Gunnar said, and let out a loud belch.

Brand motioned him to be quiet; if a lowborn claimed to be a highborn, it was a crime and punishable by flogging. Brand hadn't yet drunk enough to forget that fact.

"I don't care about smithing at all," Gunnar continued. "Only reason I kept doing it was waiting for you to quit that damnable college. Now, we can begin our journeying."

In the space of an hour, Gunnar guzzled five more horns of mead, growing dumber and dumber with each gulp. Constant rejection made even him, in his drunken state, realize that the women of the mead hall weren't going to respond to his flirtations. He and Brand left.

They hauled their drunken selves outside and into the crisp autumn air.

"Chilly, isn't it?" Brand said.

"I don't feel a thing," Gunnar said. "Besides, winter's coming."

Brand shivered at the thought. But those dark days were, indeed, coming: month after month of howling wind and endless snow. Winters in the nation of Badelgard were the worst in all human lands—not mild and rainy, like the immediate south. Because of its high elevation, even Badelgard summers required a heavy kirtle.

They wandered down the stone-cobbled roads of low-town in

the shadow of the king's residence: the famous Golden House. The fading twilight illuminated a fortune-teller who had set up a table along the road. Judging by the whiteness of her eyes, she was blind. She was human, but, judging by the carvings on the table and the strange amulets she wore, she practiced some form of Ulfr magic. All magic was illegal in Badelgard; that of the ancient Ulfr above all. Yet in Oskir—under the lax reign of King Sven—the guards looked the other way and did not bother to report sorcery or witchcraft.

Brand sat down at the fortune-teller's table. "Tell me my future, witch!" he snapped, and offered his hand.

The witch felt Brand's palm with her coarse fingers, humming as if to enter a trance. "Ah!" she called out. "There is a future planned for you. Soon—by morning's light—you will embark on a great journey, and gods alone know where the road will take you. The quest will take you to far-flung places; to places you'd never thought to travel. Yet at the end of it all… whether there are blue skies and long life, or dark shadows awaiting you, I cannot tell. Your fate is veiled in mist."

Brand looked at the witch for a few seconds, surprised by her grand prediction. "Thank you," he finally said, and giggled. He turned to Gunnar. "It's your turn."

"I will not take advice from an Ulfr witch," Gunnar said. "The Ulfr were killed long ago, and it is a shame that one of our people practice their cruel rites!" Gunnar's neck had flushed red. "The Ulfr were the most evil race the world has ever known. The things they did were against nature. Until the Dragon—praise his green scales—burned them all away."

"Can we not learn from them, also?" the blind witch said. "They were cruel to us; and yet, perhaps they have something to offer us."

"Lies!" Gunnar shouted.

"Calm yourself," Brand said, and stood up from the table. "It's just a fun little game." He brushed Gunnar's back reassuringly, then turned to the witch. "Gunnar gets angry when he's drunk!"

He guided Gunnar away from the witch, and stumbled further

down into low-town.

"We must go to The Lily House," Gunnar said. "What's the point of drinking mead if there are no women around?"

"Settle down," Brand said. "You've had a little too much, friend."

"Don't talk down to me, boy!" Gunnar said.

A king's man stood just a few yards distant. Brand could tell he was a king's man because he was dressed in steel chainmail—a costly item beyond the means of any lowborn or lesser highborn. Over his armor he wore a shirt that bore the royal Oster coat-of-arms: a gold rooster against a red field.

Gunnar stumbled close to the king's man, then let out a loud belch and stared at him dizzily. Brand walked up behind his friend and grabbed his hand. He tried to drag him away, but Gunnar was too heavy for Brand to move him.

"What are you looking at, lowborn?" the king's man sneered.

"I am not lowborn!" Gunnar shouted.

Brand winced and struck him hard. This could only end badly, and it woke Brand totally out of any drunkenness the mead had granted him. They were in serious danger, now.

"You aren't lowborn?" said the king's man mockingly. "Then pray tell, milord, why you are dressed in rags and wield a crude axe."

"This axe has served me well," Gunnar said. "It has felled many men."

"I'm sorry, milord!" Brand shouted to the king's man. "He is drunk and doesn't know what he's talking about."

"No, no; I'm very interested in him," the king's man said. "Tell me—"

"Gunnar."

"—Gunnar, what noble line you belong to," the king's man finished.

"I am Gunnar, son of Magnus Blackhelm!"

Nausea seized Brand.

"Ah! So you are the son of a great earl, and Brynja is your mother, I assume? Then why are you spending time with this miserable fop here?"

"Brynja is not my mother," Gunnar snarled. "My mother is Gertha, daughter of Agnar, and she... at one time... was a whore!" He belched again.

"So you accuse the honorable Lord Magnus Blackhelm of whoring?" said the king's man. He drew out his long steel sword, a weapon worth countless amounts of silver that only rich men could afford.

"My lord, we apologize!" Brand said. "He is drunk! He isn't capable of reason right now..."

"No lowborns are capable of reason," said the king's man. "Only the highborns can reason. Do you agree?"

"Yes, milord!" Brand said. "Please... I beg of you. Forgive us for our rudeness."

Gunnar was glaring. He had drawn out his axe. "If it's a fight you want, highborn, then you'll get one."

"Gunnar, stop!" Brand said, now in tears. But no sooner had the words left his lips than Gunnar swung down and slashed the wrist of the king's man.

Shocked, he stumbled back and gasped. Blood was spurting out of the wound like water from a broken dam. A red spray began to discolor the cobbled road. If the king's man did not die of hemorrhage, he would—in all likelihood—die of a festering wound.

"*Gunnar!*" Brand screamed. "Have you lost your mind?"

Gunnar stumbled backward dizzily. "Aye, lad," he rasped. "I think I have. I think I—" He touched his head. "We must get out of here, now."

Neither Gunnar nor Brand owned horses. But they needed horses to escape and they did not have coin to buy them. They ran up to the hostler in the Oskir Stables. Gunnar pitched back his axe—its bit still dripping with blood—as he grabbed the short, timid man by the scruff of his neck. "Give me a horse," Gunnar said, his eyes wide for fearful effect, "or I swear by the God of Death that I worship, I will send your head flying."

"Yes, milord!" the little man whimpered. "You may have Biscuit and Thimble!"

"They'd better be the fastest you have," Gunnar said, widening his eyes even further, "or I swear, I will come back here to this very stable and I won't cut your head off—I'll peel you like an apple!"

"Okay!" the little man squealed. "You can have Lightning and Hellion."

As soon as they had mounted, they galloped through the streets at a breakneck pace. The people of Oskir stared at them in confusion. Why were these two well-liked, upstanding citizens making off like outlaws? The answer, of course, was Gunnar's drinking.

"Where do we go?" Brand said, almost weeping as the horse made its way up out of low-town.

With one stupid mistake, Gunnar had ruined Brand's life as a skald. If they survived, Brand would forevermore be a criminal; a wolf to be hunted wherever he went. And, as a lowborn, Brand would face torture before the execution. A trip to the rack, the burning of his flesh, or the removal of his fingernails, would come before the mercy-stroke of the headsman's sword.

As they raced out of the Golden Gate and into the forest of firs and spruces, they caught sight of a bandit-hunting party forming: king's men dressed in the Oster coat-of-arms shirts. Instead of Gunnar's light tunic, they wore chainmail; in their hands they carried swords, and on their backs were bows and arrows. If they caught up to Brand and Gunnar, they would stand no chance.

"You are such a fool, Gunnar!" Brand cried as they galloped into the open.

"I know!" Gunnar shouted, his eyes sad yet still shallow with drunk stupidity. "I don't know what's going on, but I know I've made a horrible mistake."

"I should blame it all on you and let the torturers have you! Gods, I should do that!" Brand said. "But—by the valkyries—you are my friend, and I'm not going to betray you." He threw a cautious glance to the straw-covered stall. "Are you fit to ride? Or are you too drunk?"

"I can ride when I'm drunk," Gunnar said. "In fact, I ride better."

They were heading north on the path, and neither of them knew where they were going.

"Name a place that no man wants to go!" Gunnar thundered, bouncing in his saddle at the horse's gallop. "A place where not even king's men will dare to tread!"

"I can only think of one place the High King dares not tread," Brand said, "and that is Blackfold."

A shiver visibly passed through Gunnar's spine. "Be still my heart!" he said. "The land of ghosts… home of Ulfr magic! It is twenty miles away. I can't bear the thought of entering that place—and yet—if that is what it takes to survive… then let us go."

They guided their horses down a northeastward path. They rode at full gallop toward Blackfold, that accursed land of ghosts that even fully-armored king's men would not dare enter. At the thought of it, Brand's stomach twisted to knots.

CHAPTER TWO

Gunnar raced up the northeastern-leading path on his horse. Brand galloped just a few feet behind. It was sunrise and Blackfold was within reach.

Sven's agents pressed after them fast, hot on their trail. The High King wanted their heads. But once they left the jurisdiction, clan law would force Sven's men to stop their pursuit. Besides, no sane man wanted to enter Blackfold, birthplace of witchcraft and magic, den of wolves and wolfish men, and heavy under the weight of a dark curse.

Gunnar could see the Black River in the distance, flowing down from the mountains. The silt beneath the water gave it its color. Beyond lay Blackfold. Legend has it that three hundred years ago, the Ulfr gave the invaders such a powerful Evil Eye that they could not cross the river. A few intrepid warriors built a bridge that did not touch the water; they entered Blackfold and were massacred.

Soon Gunnar and Brand arrived at the shore of the Black River. Gunnar's horse bucked and whinnied; it would not enter the water. Brand's horse would not even get that close. The beasts were afraid of what lay beyond.

A loud horn sounded from behind; Sven's agents pressed them hard.

"It's time to swim!" Gunnar shouted and quickly dismounted.

Brand dismounted shortly afterward and then they began to swim across the Black River, through the swiftly-flowing dark waters. Finally, sopping wet, they arrived in the accursed region of Blackfold.

The region was covered in hills—not huge, mountainous hills but small ones, giving the grassy earth a rough texture.

"What now?" Brand said as they ran in.

"We stay here," Gunnar answered. "We lie low a while. Hope Sven forgets. I do not want to leave the homeland; I am a son of

Badelgard as you are. I cannot imagine going into the weaklings' lands: the farmers' fields, the soft cities of luxury...

"The outlanders would not accept a Badelgarder, anyway."

"You speak truth."

A flock of crows flew by, calling out in their hideous voices. Gunnar loosed his axe from his back and gripped it in his right hand. He shook his weapon and cursed the black-feathered crows, the most hated of birds.

"Look!" Brand said. "I see smoke! A fire—a campfire— something!"

Gunnar looked around. He spotted smoke coming from a nearby forest. "It must be a camp," he said. "Let's go."

In the pine forest was a gathering of tents. A dozen men and women sat around a large, bright-burning fire. They had on worn clothing that might have once been finely tailored, but now was patched-up, coming apart at the seams. Several wooden chests, doubtlessly full of gold and treasure, were strewn about the camp. These were bandits.

The leader, a brawny blond-haired man with a sword, walked up to them.

"If you're looking for gold, we don't have any," Gunnar said. "We're running from the law like you."

"You should never have come to this place," the man answered him. "Blackfold is cursed, and more accursed than the gossip states."

"Then why are you still here?" said Gunnar.

"High King Sven is after us for theft; Blackfold is the only place we could escape to. If Sven found me he'd give me the bloody eagle. He'd do that to all of us. But if we recover the Idol of the Great Mother, he'd forgive us for our deeds. He'd let us keep the gold we got." The man spat. "But we've learned getting the idol is going to be hard, if not impossible. The land's curse is so great we are lucky to have survived this long. A witch still haunts the barrows... she calls ghosts down upon us.

We used to have children with us; the ghosts ate their souls and we had to bury them in this haunted earth. The witch is one of the Ulfr; she is a necromancer of great power."

"The Ulfr died out long ago," said Brand.

"This one still remains," answered the bandit leader. "She keeps the Idol of the Great Mother in her den on Haunted Hill.

"What is the Idol of the Great Mother?" asked Brand. "It sounds familiar. I might have heard about it at the Skalds' College."

"You probably have," the bandit leader said. "The Ulfr did not revere the gods or the Green Dragon; they worshipped the Great Mother, a demon. They made a golden idol of her and, when the Ulfr began to die out, the Great Mother was trapped inside her likeness. The idol holds great power. King Sven would kill to get it. As a talisman, it could grant him unthinkable power."

"And what is your name?" said Gunnar.

"People call me Morrie of High Crag," the man said.

"May we sleep here?" asked Gunnar.

"You may," said Morrie. "But beware the setting sun; nighttime is when the witch calls up the spirits of the dead to torture us. She ate the souls of our children and I wonder if we're next."

Gunnar awoke in the middle of the night. The air was cold—this far north, the air was often cold, but this felt unusual. Sickness settled into his stomach and he retched twice. He couldn't breathe. It felt like something was sitting on his chest, something very heavy. In a daze, he saw a face above him. It was blurry... he thought it might be green in color.

He retched again. He was paralyzed. He couldn't hear anything, just the sound of his pounding heart. What sorcery was this?

The face hung above him for several agonizing seconds. Then, suddenly, all the tension released. The blurriness dissipated. It was Brand's face he was looking at. Sound returned to his ears.

"Are you okay?" Brand said. "Are you all right, master? Hello? Please, answer me!"

"I'm fine," said Gunnar. He was cold and covered in gooseflesh. Outside, the rosy light of dawn glowed over the eastern hills. The moon still lingered in the morning sky.

Morrie sat at a rekindled fire, boiling something sweet in a pot, perhaps morning tea.

Gunnar breathed in and out slowly. He tried to relax all his muscles, but doing so was difficult. "I just had a scare, Brand. I just had a scare. I thought I was going to die…"

"But you didn't. Would you like to hear a song to relax yourself? Or a well-told story to soothe your nerves?"

"That's all right," said Gunnar. "I will get well soon enough."

"Anything happen last night, Morrie?" asked Gunnar.

"No." Morrie took the pot off the fire and set it into the cold, hard dirt. "We think perhaps the witch has left us."

"Well, I think Brand and I might have a look around Blackfold and see what we can find."

"Why? There are wolves… spirits of the dead…"

Brand knew that Gunnar wanted the idol for himself.

"I know that the dead walk this land," said Gunnar. He extended his axe. "But I have this."

"The dead cannot be defeated by steel. Only by magic or fervent prayer."

"I think we'll put that to the test. Right, Brand?"

"Right," Brand answered.

"There was one thing I forgot to tell you," said Morrie. "These hills… did you notice how small they are?"

"Yes," said Gunnar. "Of course."

"They are not hills," said Morrie. "All of Blackfold is a burial ground. These are barrows where the dead Ulfr rest. That is why the witch's magic is so powerful. She is a necromancer and the ghosts of the dead are everywhere here…"

"We'll be all right," Gunnar said. He left for the barrows and motioned Brand to follow.

"Aren't you a little scared?" Brand said. "The dead are watching us."

"The dead cannot fight," said Gunnar. "The dead lie in graves and rot 'til they become bare bones. The dead cannot harm the living."

"Then what do you intend to do?"

"I intend to find this witch… kill her, take the idol, and give it to King Sven. Then this land will be haunted no more. If one of the Ulfr remains here alive after three hundred years, then she hasn't learned her lesson. She hasn't learned that her people are conquered."

"Badelgard for the Badelgarders?"

"Aye," said Gunnar. "Now they said the witch has a den on a place called Haunted Hill. Let's find it."

Blackfold wasn't an especially large region, but after spending a day searching for a large hill, they found no such thing.

"We'll have to ask Morrie where it is," said Gunnar.

The sun began setting over the western horizon and a pair of wolves howled nearby. Still, Brand felt safe; Gunnar was a mighty enough warrior to deserve a skald, and a mangy pack of wolves would not stand a chance against his tempered-steel axe. They continued walking until well after the sun set and the cold air settled among the barrows, and the sky grew black. At last the sight of the pine forest and the camp appeared in their horizon.

When they found the tents they saw the fire was smoldering with gray ash. The tents were empty. The treasure chests were still there, but everyone was gone. Gunnar searched around, looking for any trace of where they had left to, but he found no clues. Then he heard Brand's voice.

"Found something!" the skald said.

"What is it?" Gunnar asked.

Brand was holding a clump of stone. Gunnar walked over and took it in his hands. A series of runes was etched onto it.

It was not Badelgard script. "What is it?" Gunnar asked.

"This is Ulfr writing," Brand said. "I learned it at the Skalds' College."

"What does it say?"

"It says, 'Return from whence you came, occupiers.' Maybe we should follow the advice."

"No. Sven will imprison us."

"The witch has been here," said Brand. "The witch from the hills. The barrow witch." He looked pale. "I don't like this. I don't like this one bit. Where could they have gone? They just disappeared. They left their clothing, their treasure, their stores of food…"

"Maybe they ran away," Gunnar said. "Maybe they're cowards… but I am Gunnar son of Magnus. I am not a coward like they are."

"Then what are we to do?"

"We sleep tonight."

"Here? Where all these people disappeared?"

"Aye. Do not worry, skald. I will protect you."

Gunnar had a bad dream that night. He dreamed his entire family back in Blackhelm Keep was murdered. He dreamed the foundations of the earth had been shaken by a dark magic. He dreamed a foul hag of the night had been elected Queen of Badelgard. He dreamed of an age-long winter, of a wolf age. Then he woke up to a gray-skied morning.

Brand was awake.

"Why are you awake?" Gunnar asked.

"I couldn't sleep last night. I managed to sleep for an hour or two, but that's it. I kept hearing sounds in the wood."

"It's just your imagination," Gunnar said. "You skalds have great imaginations; that's why you think of stories and songs."

"Most skalds don't have much imagination, these days," Brand said. "But let's get out of here, Gunnar. Let's get out of here before this land eats our souls."

"Nothing can eat our souls."

"The dead can."

"The dead are skeletons."

They left the campsite and searched again for Haunted Hill. They searched through the northeastern scrub pine forest. The Dragonteeth Mountains loomed proudly in the distance with their snowcapped peaks and purplish rock. Still they did not find Haunted Hill. All they found was a land of barrows, barren, where only crows and deer lived.

They ate from the stores of food they had taken, and fell asleep.

When they awoke, there was a great hill right in front of them. It towered above them and at the top was a spacious den of wattle and daub.

Was this Haunted Hill? Brand thought. It had to be.

"Did this hill come to us?" Gunnar said.

"That's impossible," said Brand. "We must not have seen it in the darkness."

"And what is this?" Gunnar pointed to a large stone tablet, etched with Ulfr writing. "The witch has left us another message."

Brand picked up the stone. "It says, 'You have found my home, defilers of the land, killers of the Ulfr. You have murdered almost all our people and now you want to murder me. Go ahead; slay me like a sacrificial goat. Kill the last of us and I will not stop you.'"

"She's trying to make us pity her," Gunnar said. "She's trying to manipulate us. But we can't listen."

"Do we really want to kill the last of the Ulfr?" Brand said. "Haven't we spilled enough of their blood?"

"You're listening to her lies!" Gunnar shouted. "You are a son of Badelgard like I. You are my skald. And you will listen to me."

"Aye, master."

"Don't let her work her speechcraft on you, friend."

"I won't, master."

Despite its average size, scaling Haunted Hill was among the most tiring exercises Gunnar had ever undertaken. It was like in his youth, when he climbed Hrungar Hill with his stepfather. But at last they got to the witch's den, made of wattle and daub and sticks and thick tree-branches. Now, even Gunnar could feel the chill, the evil energy, which this home exuded.

What would he find here? Gunnar wondered. He held Brand's hand just so that he wouldn't run off. Brand did not have great courage like Gunnar did.

As they got to the doorway Gunnar hesitated. He tried to put a foot inside the wicked haunt but his muscles froze up, his conscious mind held him back. His heart pounded so hard he wondered if it would explode out of his chest. His stomach fluttered. He called out, "For the glory of the Green Dragon!" and forced himself to walk in.

A wire stretched across the room and strips of human flesh hung from it, etched with Ulfr runes. Gunnar wondered if it was Morrie and the other bandits' flesh and shivered. A feathered wand sat on the floor, doubtlessly used in the witch's rituals. A child-sized straw doll, covered in runes, sat up against the stick-and-clay wall. Next to that was a wooden table with an open book of Ulfr writing. Three skulls surrounded it, peering at Gunnar with hollow eyes.

Brand hesitantly walked up to the book and began reading. "The humans have invaded the land… they have made inroads into the south and defiled the altars of the Great Mother, bringing on her Evil Eye.

They come with swords stronger than bronze, and armor that covers their bodies; despite their weapons they are ignorant and unknowledgeable. They are strong but they are dumb.

"A dark age is upon us. The Great Mother wails in her temple on the Ice Plane. The idol has been forged… we will not let harm come to our blessed mother. She will rest within the idol and never be harmed by the unclean hands of the humans. Her pink eyes will always be watching, and her Evil Eye will always be on them."

"Stop!" Gunnar shouted. "Just stop reading, right now!"

There was another doorway. A dark emanation flowed out of it: malice, anger, bitterness. It was like a bad wind, a wind you could only feel in your mind. Gooseflesh formed on Gunnar's skin and a deep chill saturated his sinews. He couldn't go in there. Not even Gunnar, son of Magnus, could enter that room.

"I have to go in!" he told himself.

There was a loud crack of thunder. Gunnar swallowed his fear and charged in.

A golden idol, shaped into the likeness of a hideous hag, sat on a table. That was the source of the anger, the evil will. Yet it was the only thing that could exonerate Gunnar of his crimes. He reached for it.

"Touch me," it said. "Touch me and free me from this prison. I promise I won't harm your soul."

"Lies!" Gunnar said. "You are just a statue, a piece of gold. You can't harm my soul."

"What makes you so sure?" it said.

The aura pulsing from the statuette almost formed a tangible wall of force. Gunnar stumbled back a step. His heart felt like it was going to rupture. He couldn't touch the idol. He couldn't take it with him. He was no match for the Idol of the Great Mother, the barrow witch's most prized possession. The Ulfr would continue on. The land of Blackfold would remain cursed until the end of time. The evil here was too great, too ancient. It would never lift, and even the gods could not lift it. No force in the universe, let alone Gunnar or Brand, could remove the curse from Blackfold.

No. It was forcing him to think like this. Gunnar peeled off his kirtle and threw the thick blue cloth around the golden idol. With the covering, some of the negativity dissipated. Then he fled out of the witch's den with Brand close behind, and ran straight south as a storm began.

They slept in the pouring rain, in the thunder and lightning. Gunnar kept the idol wrapped up in his kirtle and tried to ignore its constant emanations. He had a nightmare—and one he did not remember upon waking—but he grabbed the cloth-wrapped idol and ran on. His freedom was worth it. High King Sven could deal with this evil talisman; the king's heart was dark enough to deal with it, anyway. It was his problem. It would be his problem. And Gunnar would be free.

They exited the land from where they had entered, crossing the Black River with its dark silty waters. The storm continued in Blackfold as if the land were angry that the idol had gone. It would make a great gift to Sven, but Gunnar had no doubt that the added power would come at a steep price. He wondered what would happen to the barrow witch without her idol. He was glad she wouldn't have it.

He remembered that he had left a great treasure there, sitting in the bandit camp, but then he realized that all the treasure in the world could not get him to go back there and face the barrow witch of Blackfold.

CHAPTER THREE

The ride back to Oskir filled Brand's heart with trepidation. He wasn't sure whether Sven would accept the idol as atonement; he only knew that, in the eyes of the law, they were wolves to be hunted. They rode slightly easier through the forests of the great firs. Soon, snow would lie on their boughs, but for now, the land was green.

Oskir's proud walls appeared in the distance, as did the lights of King's Hill. Brand and Gunnar had not yet reached Golden Gate when a group of soldiers—king's men, all—rode up to them, their chainmail glinting and their swords flashing in the sunlight.

"In the name of the High King, lay down your arms!" demanded their captain, who rode in front. "You are the murderers of the king's cupbearer, Bjarni, and—by the Green Dragon—you will pay with your lives."

If these soldiers did not listen, torture and execution awaited Brand and Gunnar, who were both lowborn. "Men of great honor, I salute you," Brand said, choosing his words carefully. "Please do not arrest me; I have brought a gift of atonement for the king—something he will not pass up lightly."

"There can be no atonement for what you have done," the captain said.

"We have brought the High King a gift beyond price," Gunnar said, "an idol of Ulfr gold and a talisman of great power."

"You mean…" The captain's eyes widened.

"The Idol of the Great Mother," Brand said.

"The king's lore-masters have said much about it," the captain said. "So, too, have many ancient runestones told of its power. The wielder of the idol possesses vast strength… and Sven believes it can solidify the realm under his rule, so that none may rebel." For a moment his eyes reflected unbelief. "Show it to me."

Gunnar unraveled the idol from his cloak. The golden object, forged in the shape of an old crone, was carved with eerie realism.

The captain's eyes widened further, as did those of his men. "Very well, boy. I do not know if Sven Oster can ever forgive you for what you've done. But I will see if he wishes to grant audience with you. If he cannot find it in his heart to forgive, it's off to the torturer for you."

In the end, Sven did grant audience with them. The king's Golden House was richly furnished: there were purple drapes over all the windows, beeswax layering the wooden floors, and paintings of brilliant color hanging on the walls.

The High King himself sat on a great oaken throne which itself was hemmed with gold. He had a thick, reddish-brown beard and dark eyebrows. On his head was a crown of purple velvet and jewel-studded gold.

"You are wolves, murdering wolves," Sven said. "You killed my cupbearer."

Brand fell to his knees. Gunnar unraveled the idol from his cloak and threw it onto the floor.

Suddenly Sven's eyes glinted with wonder, and a little bit of greed. "Oh, my. You have done well," he muttered, eyeing the ornate object with wide eyes. "Bring it to me."

There was no mercifulness or compassion in his dark green eyes—and, had they offered anything of lesser value than the Idol of the Great Mother, there would be no forgiveness in them either.

"Here it is, my king." Gunnar picked up the idol, walked over to the king, and placed it into his grasp. "It is my great privilege to deliver it into such worthy hands."

"It is hard for a king to forgive, and some may say, unfitting," Sven said, rubbing the cold metal of the idol. "But you have done me a great service. Now that I have it, I will have great power." A slight smile crept over his features as he continued to stroke the idol.

"Are we free of our crimes?" Brand asked.

"My dear friend Henrik is the lord of the Frostfall marches. Do you read?"

Gunnar shook his head. "No, my king."

Sven's cunning green eyes turned to Brand. "And you?"

"No," Brand lied.

"It is no matter," Sven said. From the folds of his sable-lined robe, he pulled a sealed vellum scroll. "My dear friend Henrik is the marcher lord, and an important man to our proud nation's defense. He needs men… and—if I judge your profession correctly boy—those men need skalds. If you will bring this letter to him and promise to serve him for as long as he needs you, I will absolve you of your crimes."

"How long will that be?" Brand asked.

"A year, at most," Sven said.

"And if we refuse?" Gunnar said.

Sven laughed. "If you do not deliver it, I will put you back on the Hangman's List. I will find the best torturers in the country and I will give you a slow, slow death. Do you understand?"

"Yes," Gunnar grunted.

Sven's expression darkened. "If you do not obey me, then— believe me—I will find out and haunt you to your grave."

Both Gunnar and Brand believed him.

Having no horses, the duo hiked for two days across mountainous, heavily-wooded terrain. They would hike two more before they got to Frostfall, the northernmost region of all Badelgard, where it snowed even in summer and, in winter, was unnavigable.

That night, in the scarce warmth of the campfire, Gunnar raged at untrustworthiness of Sven. Sven was not trustworthy, neither as a High King nor as a man. "We should open the letter," Gunnar said. "You can read it."

"Open the letter?" Brand laughed incredulously. "If we break the seal, we will be committing a crime. Sven's friend will behead us."

Gunnar scratched his beard in thought. "I do not trust Sven's intentions."

"That makes two of us," Brand said. "But we can't risk it, milord."

"You're right. We cannot risk it." Gunnar took the scroll and broke the seal.

"Why did you do that, Gunnar?" Brand asked.

He shot Brand a stern look and handed him the scroll. "Read."

"My dear friend," Brand read, "Because of my great affection toward you and for the benefit of our eternal friendship, I grant you permission to sacrifice these two lowborns. –Sven."

Gunnar grunted. "Next time, listen to me when I do not trust a person's intentions."

"Yes, friend," Brand said, gazing into the fire with concern. "What shall we do now? Shall we leave Badelgard?"

"I cannot imagine leaving the most honorable of nations," Gunnar said. He snatched the letter, crumpled it up, and threw it into the flame. "We are in the Trowheim region and—though it is heavily wooded—surely there is a safe town here."

"There is no safe town," Brand said. "Blackhelm Keep is not far away, but the earl does not harbor outlaws."

"We do not change our course, then. We go to Frostfall," Gunnar said. "There are caves in the sides of the mountains. My friend Ivarr—Green Dragon guard him—was a deserter from the king's army. His battalion was attacked by White Wolves and he was the only smart one; he ran away. They wanted to execute him as a coward, but he ran away and hid in the Frostfall caves for many years."

"What happened to him?"

Gunnar frowned. "Eventually he couldn't take the silence and loneliness, and the cold of Frostfall. He left and made for Oskir. I had the chance to get drunk with him one last time before the king's men got to them. He had his thumbnails ripped out… then they sent him off to the gallows, and had him hanged."

Brand shivered.

By sunset of the next day, the great green pines of Trowheim were behind them. They entered the high country: the rocky Ice Shelf which jutted from the mountains as a plateau. It was a pure sheet of ice. There were no elks, deer, or hares to eat, and thus no wolves. Eons ago, trolls walked this plateau and conspired with the Ulfr before the proud sons and daughters of Badelgard drove both races to extinction.

A thick layer of ice covered every inch of the Shelf and the winds blew from every direction, knifing into every exposed part of Brand's body, despite the fact that he wore a heavy fur coat. In the darkness, having no wood for a fire, Gunnar and Brand huddled together against the wailing winds. The night lasted what seemed like an age. By morning, neither had slept more than an hour and both were frozen to the innermost sinew. Stiffly, they continued across the Ice Shelf, occasionally slipping, with Gunnar in the lead and providing direction.

They reached the drop-off in the twilit hours of late afternoon. They carefully climbed down the hard, icy rock and set foot on the grassland that made up Frostfall. It was not much warmer here, though the wind was less severe. Even now, in mid-autumn, patches of snow lay across the grassland. Many miles west lay the lowlands, the sea, and the large town of Andarr's Port. To the north was White Wolf Keep, home of Sven's brother, and a few leagues past that were the borderlands. To the east—where Gunnar planned to go, were the hundreds of caves, obscured by a dense pine forest full of game.

They reached those caves in the middle of the night.

CHAPTER FOUR

Brand awoke to a hard kick and a sword point pressed against his neck. The blurred figure of a bandit towered above him.

"Who are you?" Brand gasped.

As his vision cleared, he realized that it was not the heavy-set figure of a man before him, but the lithe shape of a woman.

"You shouldn't sleep with your guard down," she said in a cheerful voice. "You're lucky you're not carrying anything, or it'd be off with your head."

"What is your name?" As Brand's eyes further adjusted to the light, he noticed that Gunnar was relaxed, sitting against the cave wall, and sharpening his axe.

The bandit was dressed in men's clothing: crudely-cut leather leggings, a leather jerkin and thin woolen gloves. Yet her facial features were clearly feminine, and a set of thick, strawberry-blonde hair flowed down her back.

One thing about her struck Brand as strange: running down her cheeks were twin white scars. They would be the great pride of any fighting man, and could only have been gained through battle, or the purposeful cutting of a blade.

"I am Hilda," the woman said confidently. "I come from the village of Skotja near the King's Drawbridge. I am hiding from the law like you and your skald."

"What crime did you commit?"

She ignored the question and locked toward Gunnar. She pointed to a pile of logs on the cave floor. "I got some firewood from the forest. Make yourself useful and get a fire going."

"I do not take commands from a woman," Gunnar said.

"Men," Hilda said. "You're all the same. I had high hopes for you, since your skald is such a nice boy." She kicked Gunnar in the gut and blocked an axe-strike. "Get working."

She is a tough woman, Brand thought. *The scars running across her cheeks are not the only scars she bears.*

In his own time, Gunnar did gather some kindling from the forest and start a fire with Hilda's tinderbox. Together, the three of them sat around the crackling flames and reveled in the warmth.

"Now that I've done as you asked, like a servant, perhaps you can tell me your story," Gunnar said. "Why are you hiding in these caves, Hilda?"

"My crimes are too numerous to mention," Hilda said. "I have stolen; I have killed. But perhaps, above all, the reason why the earls' men hunt me with such a vengeance is because I do not accept my 'place' as a woman. I do not let men stuff me in a little dress and tell me what to do. I wear the clothing of men, I make my own decisions, and I fight my own battles."

"Your story is worthy of a song," Brand said.

Hilda laughed. "I put no stock in songs or fables. But thank you, skald."

"And what of those scars on your face? Did you gain them from fighting?" Gunnar said.

"No," Hilda said. She shot Gunnar a smile, but it was a sad, weary smile. "The story of the scars starts when I was young. My father is highborn. He is of the House Summerleaf. He is very ambitious, and forced me to marry a horse chief from outside Badelgard. He wanted the alliance so he could use the horse peoples' strength to overthrow the High King. Well, I was just thirteen at the time. I was scared and desperately did not want to marry him. The wedding night was a trauma. I would call it a rape even though I did not struggle against him. He was like an animal, without any kind of tenderness or romance. I was an object to bear his children."

The lack of emotion in her voice startled Brand.

"He was horrible to behold," she continued, "and he smelled like horse dung. The horse chiefs don't bathe very often, you see."

"And the scars?" Brand said.

Hilda touched her cheek. "The horse chiefs cut their wives as part of the marriage ceremony—it's a symbol of total submission. Cowards, thieves, murderers—they care less about criminals than women who refuse to submit to their husbands. A woman who does not submit is considered worse than a murderer. Even then, at that tender age, I did not like the restrictions on my sex."

She looked down in thought. "I was still rebellious. After the wedding night, I tried to run away twice. Both times, they caught me and beat me until I truly realized that I had to submit. These horsemen were too numerous for me to rebel against, and the women had no sympathy on me, either. So I gave up for six years and let him have me... I bore the bedeviled churl three daughters. He was displeased I had not borne him any proper male heirs to the chiefdom and thought I was a 'witch-woman.' They thought they'd burn me at the stake, but Harram—my husband—had compassion on me, took his tribesmen and rode off. He took my daughters with him."

"What happened after that?"

"I returned to Skotja. My father was so disappointed in me that he tried to have me killed; by now I was so hardy that I overcame his men and killed them both. I was sentenced to be drawn and quartered. I escaped and rode off west... Now I'm on the Hangman's List. I heard of these caves and met with some outlaws... they are gone now, though."

"Where are they?" asked Brand.

"They left last week." Hilda stared into the flames. "The earl, Henrik, has said that any man—including outlaws on the Hangman's List—can come serve him at White Wolf Keep without fear of penalty, if they pledge loyalty. As a woman, I am excluded."

"Are you sure they would not include you?" Gunnar asked.

"No," Hilda said. "But in the low chance he delivers me back to my father, my father will beat me and have me killed; and that is a chance

I will not take."

"Do you want to take revenge on your father?" Brand asked.

A hint of anger grew in Hilda's eyes. "Like hell I do."

Hilda left shortly after their conversation and returned an hour later with a dead snowshoe hare. By now the fire had died down slightly and both Gunnar and Brand were huddled around it. Even here, below the Shelf, the air was far colder than in Oskir. As Hilda flayed and removed the meat from the dead rabbit, a light rain began.

"You've been through much," Gunnar said. "I understand if you never want to be in a man's presence again. But I—and surely, Brand as well—want to pledge service to Lord Henrik. It would be safe. There'd be warmth and food in White Wolf Keep."

Brand glanced at the raw rabbit-flesh.

"If you come with us, I will protect you, "Gunnar said. "I will not touch you in any unfitting way. I will guard you, and—I swear an oath to the Green Dragon—if they try to send you back to your father I will guard you against them and escape with you."

"I don't need your help," Hilda said. "You both seem to be good men and that is so very rare. I will go with you to White Wolf Keep, but not because of you... not because I trust you. I will go because I was looking for an excuse to go. Every other person here has left, including the women. I was being overcautious."

They set out early the next morning. They broke through the dense forest and a steep, rocky ascent began that took Brand's breath away and made his legs sore. An hour or so later, the ascent stopped and the ground became more level, if uneven. Before them was a rocky brown plain that stretched on as far as they could see.

"We've reached the Frostfall Highlands," Hilda said. "Elk are here in abundance; so are White Wolves. You'd best pray we never run into those."

Hilda went on to explain that the men of Frostfall had both fear and respect for White Wolves: fear because they sometimes attacked humans and because only the strongest of warriors could defeat them in combat; and respect because, in ancient days, their chief Snowpelt had made a temporary alliance with the humans against the Ulfr, who often used their hearts in rituals.

The sun had not yet set when the tall wooden walls of White Wolf Keep (named, Brand presumed, out of respect) appeared in the horizon. And they had not yet come within a half a mile of it when a dozen armored men on equally-armored horses rode out to meet them, one of whom bore the keep's standard: a silver wolf against a blue field, flapping in the harsh Frostfall winds.

"State your business!" said a rider with a large brown moustache and a shaven chin. Around his helmet was a golden band. "What are you doing in Frostfall, the northernmost march?"

"We come to pledge our utmost loyalty to the marcher lord!" Brand shouted.

Gunnar grunted in agreement.

"You are speaking to the marcher lord," the rider said. "I am Henrik Silverback, earl of Frostfall."

Brand sighed at his own stupidity. The golden band—the equivalent of a coronet—should have given it away.

"Are you outlaws?" Lord Henrik said.

"Yes!" Hilda shouted with surprising enthusiasm. "We come according to your statement that you seek soldiers. We pledge ourselves utterly in your service."

"And what about you?" Lord Henrik said, looking at Gunnar. "Do you also pledge yourself in my service?"

"Yes." After a moment's hesitation, Gunnar dropped to his knees and bowed his head. Hilda and Brand followed a second later.

Henrik touched Gunnar's head with the flat of his spearhead. "You will be my soldier." He glanced at Brand. "Judging by your instruments, you will be my skald." He turned his eyes to Hilda. "You. You are a scarred woman. You hold a spear. You'd not make a good mistress and, by the looks of you, not a spinner of wool neither. You are not permitted in White Wolf Keep."

Gunnar stood up. "I will not go unless you take her."

Henrik's eyes narrowed as he looked at Gunnar. "You are in no position to disobey me."

"If you do not take Hilda," Gunnar said, "then I will serve you half-heartedly. And a half-hearted warrior is the worst kind to have. A half-hearted soldier does not rejoice at your victories; he only serves himself."

Henrik's glare intensified. "It is unfitting for you to speak to an earl in that manner." He waved, and the riders lowered their spears. "The woman may stay if she minds her business. I'm afraid I can't afford to lose you; I need all the skilled warriors I can get."

Inside the curtain walls of White Wolf Keep was a collection of ramshackle wooden houses seriously in need of repair. Chickens, pigs, and to a lesser extent, cows, wandered the muddy, straw-covered ground and left their dumpings in the open. The people wore dull gray and brown woolen clothing. In all, it was very evident that White Wolf Keep was poor, and for obvious reasons: What resources did they have? No arable land; only pastures to create wealth.

Even the inner keep was made of wood. As they entered, it became evident that even the earl's court wore plain, undyed clothing like the populace: garments that no king's man or woman would be caught dead wearing. In the fire was a whole pig roasting on a spit, yet nothing else seemed to be cooking.

Brand and Gunnar were given a seat near the marcher lord's table. Hilda sat on the other side of the room with the keep's women. Brand and Gunnar were each given plain drinking-horns. One taste and it became clear they were serving bitter dark ale; not the heavenly sweet, crisp mead of Oskir.

As the smell of roasting pig filled the room, Gunnar walked up to Henrik and bowed. "Milord," he said.

"What is it?" asked Henrik.

"A question for you," Gunnar said. "If you have been recruiting soldiers, where are they?"

Only a dozen males were in the room; half of those were servants, and the other seemed very old or very young. "They are all at war," Henrik said, "just as you will be tomorrow. I've sent them east—"

"East? Near the mountains?" Gunnar asked. "Why do you need soldiers there?"

"I cannot tell you," answered Henrik. "Too many have run away when I told them, and though I suspect you are a brave man, Gunnar, I do not know just how brave you are. I will only state that the men at the watchtower on the edge of the Darkling Wood in the northeast need help. They need your axe, Gunnar."

"Why?" asked Gunnar.

"It is of dire importance," Henrik said. "If I left the watchtower unmanned, I would be a poor marcher lord indeed." He paused. "The girl stays. I am sure she possesses some talent that will be useful to me, such as spinning, and if she does not, we can teach her," Henrik said. "The scars will frighten men off... but perhaps there is a place for her if there is no man for her."

"She is a warrior," Gunnar said. "She could come with us and fight."

"Dragon knows, the men at the watchtower are starved for women, and bad enough for a woman as gruff as Hilda," Henrik said, "but we of Frostfall would never let even a common whore from a port brothel face the evil there. Nor would we force a woman to fight."

"What if she wants to fight?" Gunnar asked.

"Then by Vana's harp, she is an aberration indeed," Henrik said. "She is not going with you, Gunnar, even if she wants to. It is not the

Frostfall way."

That night Brand played the lute and sang the song of Badelgard's genesis.

Our father, Lord Buntringer, climbed the Sky Cliffs with his hands
He dropped a sturdy rope down, helped his sons go claim the land

Three sons he had by Aelwin, blessed mother of our race:
Hjarta, Himnall, Helgur all saw the Ulfr's great disgrace

The Ulfr wed their sisters, and their women cast dark spells
They offered up their children, and trolls were on the fells

Only the Green Dragon—let all men praise his name—
Could kill the Ulfr witches with his powerful red flame

At once Lord Henrik shouted, "You stay with me, skald. Your voice is as pure as honey and your fingers quick as White Wolves in full sprint!"

Brand did not want to leave Gunnar, but an earl's words were law.

By now, Gunnar had fallen asleep from the mead. He had good dreams of the Green Dragon and the white-garbed goddess of victory, Vana, and woke in good spirits; but sensed that good spirits were not commonplace in the Darkling Wood, where he would go.

CHAPTER FIVE

At dawn, Lord Henrik gave Gunnar a white mare named Snowbell. The fletcher gave Gunnar fifty arrows, and the bowyer gave Gunnar a finely-strung bow of mountain yew. The blacksmith offered him a leather jerkin with the symbol of White Wolf Keep stitched onto it.

"No," Gunnar refused. "Armor slows a man down."

Then Gunnar hopped on Snowbell and followed an escort through the open gate. He followed the escort through the cold, windy plains of Frostfall for perhaps two hours when the Darkling Wood appeared in the horizon. A wooden wall blocked entrance. Yet stretching above the wall were tall pines—dark green, almost black against the steely gray peaks of the mountains. Not far off in the distance was an impossibly tall wooden watchtower, and gathered behind it were numerous tents and perhaps a dozen men, outfitted with swords, spears, bows, and other weaponry.

The escort left him as soon as he reached the camp. The dozen men were gathered around a large campfire, roasting haunches of meat in the bright flames.

"Greetings!" Gunnar thundered. Snowbell stopped her trot.

A man in an iron breastplate got up from the campfire. A scar ran across the length of his face and his nose was crooked, perhaps broken. He had thick, dirty blond hair and light blue eyes. "You are the new man, eh?" he said. "I am Captain Jannik. Have some elk skewers. You'll need your full strength when you go in the Darkling Wood tonight."

"Why night?" Gunnar said. "Surely that is the most dangerous time for an expedition. In morning I can see well."

"Aye," Jannik said. "But night is when the evil is gone. We sent two men last night—Agni and Rannulf—to find the source of the evil in the woods. They've not come back. We need you to go there and find them and rescue them before the evil takes them."

"Your men have legs, Jannik, and so do you. You are not cripples. So why are you sending me? Why aren't you sending these others?"

The men around the campfire looked up at Gunnar and glared at him.

Jannik walked up to Gunnar and put a hand on his shoulder. "The darkness has taken them. If they go into the Darkling Wood, they will become part of the evil in the woods. They were not careful when they entered the forest. They let the curse touch them." He looked at Gunnar grimly. "If they stray from the fire... if they get too cold, they will succumb."

A chill ran up Gunnar's spine, worse than the harshest ice-throes of winter. "And what about you? Why don't you go with me?"

"The watchtower needs a captain," Jannik answered. "Without a captain these men will die, and if they die, the evil will flood the wall, and there will be no hope for White Wolf Keep, and no hope for all Badelgard."

The sun set in a dazzling display of gold and red. A White Wolf howled in the mountains, heralding the coming night. Fully armed, Gunnar unsheathed his sword and rode Snowbell through the vast wooden gate. He took one look back and Jannik was staring at him, eyes mournful as if he were watching a man going to his death.

CHAPTER SIX

They came with fire and steel.
They came on dragon's back.
They called our customs vile
They killed us to the last.

As Brand sang the last bit of the famous song, "Lament of the Ulfr," the sound of applause filled the main hall of White Wolf Keep. In the Skalds' College, Brand had not been the best student, not by any means. But these rustic northerners were not used to good entertainment, only war, dull clothing, and constant cold. Compared to the amateurs they were used to, Brand was a musical genius.

"Thank you," he said, and bowed.

The ladies were looking upon him with fawning expressions. The men seemed equally enthralled. Only Hilda looked unmoved, focused solely on eating her porridge.

"You've done well," Lord Henrik called out from his throne. "Perhaps if we sent you to fight the evil in the Darkling Wood, you could vanquish it with the purity of your voice."

"Milord," Brand said. "Forgive me for prying, but you have sent my best friend to fight the evil there. Just what is this evil?"

"It's nothing!" Lord Henrik said. "He will be back soon. Now, play on! Play a song of fear... a song of horrors and dark times. Make my hairs stand on end."

"Very well," Brand said. He began strumming his lute to the sound of the song "Fell Winter."

A winter will fall over Badelgard
A winter that never ends
Children will die of hunger
And the Ulfr, crawl up from their dens

And the Ulfr, crawl up from their dens

Ice will fall from the heavens
The dead will return from their stones
The starving will feed on each other
And a corpse shall sit on the throne
And a corpse shall sit on the throne

Men will abandon honor
Kin will turn against kin
Snow-age, dark-age, White Wolf-age
'til the Ulfr have their revenge
'til the Ulfr have their revenge

The applause returned. Lord Henrik clapped and cheered the loudest of the lot. But Hilda stood up and shouted, "How dare you sing of such things?" then stormed out of the hall.

"One moment," Brand said. He set his lute against the wall and ran after Hilda, following her outside into the windy night.

"I am sorry, lady," Brand said.

"I am not a lady," Hilda said. "I have killed men before. Have you?"

"No," Brand said. "But it's just a song—it isn't a prophecy. At least, most people don't think it's a prophecy."

"Where did you learn it?" Hilda snapped.

"The headmaster at the Skalds' College taught it to me," Brand said. "He heard a madman singing it in Andarr's Port and wrote it down. It means nothing. Surely a man who has no grip on reality cannot speak truth."

"Don't you think singing that is treasonous to the sons and

daughters of Badelgard?" Hilda shouted. "It celebrates the Ulfr, who used human hearts in their rituals—who ate the flesh of men and women both. They worshiped a demoness, The Great Mother!"

"I hate the Ulfr as much as you do, if not more," Brand said. "I have been to the land of Blackfold. I have been in the house of an Ulfr witch. Can you say the same?"

"I do not know where Blackfold is," Hilda said. "I assume it is in the east."

"It is the most haunted land in all Badelgard."

"I doubt it," Hilda said. "I believe Gunnar has gone to the most haunted land in Badelgard."

"What do you mean?"

"Agni and Rannulf were my friends," Hilda said. "They were called to the Darkling Wood. I fear for their lives. You should fear for Gunnar's life as well, but I don't."

"Why not?"

"Because he means nothing to me. He is not my friend. And he is a fool to have accepted the earl's demand."

"Perhaps if you had a heart, you would care, you cold, cruel dog," Brand said. "He is my friend. I am his skald; I am to sing of his deeds. If he dies, I must kill myself by honorary law. Don't you understand?"

Hilda frowned. "I used to be idealistic, like you. I used to believe in honor. But when Chieftain Harram raped me repeatedly and I tried to use reason with him, I realized that honor wasn't going to get me away from him. There are no valkyries watching over us. There are only three things to guide us: strength; guile; and pure, dumb luck."

"I hope I never grow as bitter as you," Brand said.

"I hope you do," Hilda said. "I hope you learn to put honor second. Because I don't want you to die. I don't want you to kill yourself if Gunnar dies, as he most certainly will. I think you're a good boy, Brand. And I think you'd be a better boy if you stop singing such vile songs."

"I am not a boy. I am a man," Brand argued.

"Musicians, storytellers," Hilda said. "A dreamer is always a child. Until you take up the sword of a warrior and pledge yourself to an earl, you will always be a boy in my eyes."

Brand glared at her. "What makes you so certain that Gunnar is going to die?"

A hint of compassion fell over Hilda's face, but she quickly hid it. "The Darkling Wood is a deadly place."

"Gunnar has survived deadly places before."

"There is evil in that forest, and the evil is hungry," Hilda said. "The darklings feed on fear and human flesh. The earl has sent Gunnar in the tiny chance he might cure the evil—so tiny it's more likely that animals learn to talk. In the infinitely more likely chance that he will die, the darklings' hunger will be sated for a while."

"So you mean to tell me that the earl sent Gunnar as a sacrifice?" Brand said incredulously.

There was no emotion in Hilda's voice as she said, "Yes."

CHAPTER SEVEN

Gunnar stood in the cold, silent forest on the other side of the wooden wall. Snow lay on the ground and on the boughs of the pines. Darkness was spreading across the sky, now. There were no owls hooting, no nightingales singing. And as Snowbell's hooves crunched against the snow, it became evident that there were no animal tracks either. If Gunnar's gut didn't tell him otherwise, he would think the forest was completely empty.

He trotted deeper in. Directly in front of him, towering above the dark pines, was an impossibly tall, snowy peak. The men of the watchtower called it Devil's Tooth.

The silence deepened as Gunnar trotted further into the forest. The silence became a sound in his ears, a constant hum.

He was a mile into the lonely forest when unease set in. His heartbeat picked up pace. A chill ran through his bones, and it wasn't caused by the snow or wind. Only after a few long minutes in that heightened state did he see anything.

In the distance were two humanoid figures, leaning against the trunk of a pine. Gunnar kicked the stirrups and trotted up to them. One of the figures was an adult woman and the other was a young boy of no more than four or five. Both were lifeless and frozen solid, their eyes dead and glassy. The woman had her arm rigidly wrapped around the child's shoulder; the child's right hand was solid as an icicle against the woman's waist. The woman's stomach was swollen and distended; Gunnar would have thought that she was with child, had the boy's stomach not been similarly swollen. Death did strange things to bodies.

Gunnar gave a passing thought to giving them a burial. But there were more important matters at hand than the dead. He had to find the two missing soldiers, Agni and Rannulf, and these were not soldiers.

They were mother and child—innocent, harmless creatures whom Lady Vana had not smiled upon or protected with her valkyries. He kicked the stirrups and trotted away.

Snowbell's breath turned to fog in the cold as she huffed and trotted quickly through the forest toward Devil's Tooth. Gunnar looked around as the darkness fell. From the looks of it, the Darkling Wood was only about a mile in length and two miles wide. He would find Agni and Rannulf—or their corpses—very soon.

Gunnar's heartbeat was audible against the silence. So was Snowbell's. "Agni? Rannulf?" he shouted at the top of his lungs, more to break the silence than receive a response.

There was a loud howl from the mountains. Gunnar could tell it belonged to a White Wolf due to its loudness and purity of tone. He drew his axe.

"Agni? Rannulf?" he shouted again.

He looked to his left and his heart went cold. There, frozen standing up and leaning against a large tree trunk, were the bodies of two grown men. One had a thick brown beard and the other, a thin blonde one. Both wore steel armor emblazoned with the standard of White Wolf Keep—the same breastplate that the blacksmith had offered Gunnar. In their lifeless, frozen hands were swords of a non-Frostfallian make. These had to be Agni and Rannulf.

Gunnar hesitated. Their eyes were lifeless, but he felt their gazes on him. He swallowed his unease and dismounted. Slowly, he walked up to them. He grabbed the brown-bearded man's sword. He tried to pull it out of the frozen, lifeless fingers. He pulled again but it didn't budge. He yanked hard with a sharp cry and the icy fingers cracked and fell off onto the ground.

The sword had the "AP" runes of Andarr's Port. He glanced over to the other one. The blond man's sword had the "BH" runes of Blackhelm Keep. They were not locals; they were recruits for the watchtower. Gunnar could not read books or scrolls but after a long warrior's life under the service of many lords, he recognized the many keeps' runes.

After a struggle, he ripped the sword from the other corpse's fingers. This time, he broke off the entire hand and removed the iced-on limb with a hard struggle.

The darkness was complete, now, and Gunnar wanted to go home. At the least, he wanted to go to the campfire near the watchtower. He hopped on Snowbell and noticed, in the dim light of the moon, that the two corpses were smiling. Nauseous, Gunnar went away at a brisk canter, swords bundled in his left hand.

The White Wolf howled again.

He had ridden scarcely ten yards when the woman and child from before were back in view, leaning against a different tree trunk. Gunnar gulped. Sensing his trembling heart, he shouted, "I will slay every demon and ghoul in this forest. I know you hear me, devil! Enjoy your last few moments."

He dismounted, ran over to the frozen woman, and slammed the bit of his axe into her skull. Her head split in two frozen parts and fell to the ground. He hesitated with the child, but reminded himself this was a demon, not a boy. He slashed sideways with as much force as he could muster and sent the child's head flying. Next, he cut off both corpses' legs.

"Now you can't move, devils."

The boy's head spoke as it rolled across the snow. A voice—childish yet cold as a snake's eyes—said, "Neither will you."

Blood sprayed Gunnar from behind. He turned around, heart pounding loud as a drum. Agni and Rannulf were there. In the blond man's hands was Snowbell's torn-off head.

"I'll gut you like an elk!" Gunnar screamed.

Both Agni and Rannulf were smiling, and blood rimmed their mouth. Without hesitation Gunnar kicked them both to the ground, slashed off their heads, and then chopped off their feet and hands. He prayed to Eliane, horse goddess, that she would give Snowbell eternal rest. He dropped the swords. Then he asked all the gods who'd listen if they'd save him, as he took off toward the gate at a dead sprint.

He reached the gate exhausted. His heart raced so fast he worried it might rupture. He pounded on the gate. He dropped his axe and beat the gate with both hands.

"Open!" he screamed. "Open up!"

He looked back. More dead had followed them to the gate, all frozen and staring at him with cocked heads and smiling, hungry lips.

"Open!" he screamed even louder. "Open, now, or I swear…"

He looked back. The dead had drawn closer. A figure in a black cloak walked out of the shadows toward him, moving across the snow yet leaving no footprints. Protruding from the sleeves were long, withered green fingers.

"You vicious human warrior," a woman's voice said from inside the cloak. "Why have you harmed my children?"

Lining her hood were Ulfr runes.

CHAPTER EIGHT

In the middle of the night, Brand awoke short of breath. He had a nightmare, one which he could not remember. One thing he knew, though; he had to go to the watchtower and save Gunnar even if it was a losing battle. Quietly, he got up from his bed and threw on his fur cloak. He packed his lute and what little provisions he had into a sack. Then, with as much silence as he could muster, he left through the door, tiptoed past the earl's chambers, crept down the stairs, and peered into the main hall.

The two guards were sleeping on the chairs and snoring. Brand snuck past them and walked out of the large double doors into the cold Frostfall air. There, standing on the wooden patio that overlooked the humble gray-brown dwellings of White Wolf Keep, was Hilda.

"You're going to the Darkling Wood, aren't you?" Hilda said, looking ahead. "Crafty boy."

Brand paused. "And you? What are you doing out here on the patio?"

"My business is my concern alone, boy," Hilda said. She grasped the hilt of her sword. "You know, if you walk to the Darkling Wood, Gunnar will be long gone. The evil there will already have taken him. Only a horse will do."

"How do you know so much about the Darkling Wood, Hilda?" Brand asked.

"I've spent a long time in Frostfall," Hilda answered. "Storytellers—dreamers like you—have told me about what lies in the Darkling Wood. The evil of the Ulfr remains there, and the dead live again. If the evil does not feed, it grows hungry. And if it is hungry, it will spread past the wall. Henrik would never admit this, but the real job of the Frostfall marcher lord is to feed that evil. The half-breeds to the north do not bother us much; it is only the power of the Darkling Wood that Badelgard needs protection from."

"Perhaps it is time to fight the evil in the Darkling Wood instead of feeding it," Brand said.

"You're right, boy. But there is no hero alive today that could stop the evil in that forest. Perhaps the Green Dragon could." She turned around and looked at Brand firmly in the eye. "I'll help you find him, Brand. My former husband Harram taught me how to steal a horse… and ride one at full speed."

"I can't say the same," Brand said.

"We'll ride two-a-saddle," Hilda said.

"What made you change your mind?"

"I do not want to be bitter; nor do I wish to be a cold, cruel dog," Hilda answered. "You have a way with words, boy." As she walked down the patio steps, she said, "Also, the earl is forcing me to spin wool tomorrow and learn to be ladylike. I'd rather die fighting darklings than be a well-mannered lady."

"You are a braver man than I," Brand said.

Hilda laughed.

At the door of the lord's stables, Hilda chanted a strange song. It was in a different language—a thicker, more guttural language—and the melody was in a mode that Brand had never heard before. A horse trotted out: a shapely black mare with her mane tied into braids.

"I will name you Midnight," Hilda said, and hopped on her new steed. Brand mounted right behind her.

Hilda clucked and rode her fast out of the gate. The equerry ran out of his adjacent hovel and screamed, "Thieves! Horse thieves! An' they've taken the best one!"

Midnight galloped swiftly away from White Wolf Keep and into the stony plain. Brand was surprised at how obedient Midnight was, but Hilda had ridden with the horse peoples and knew their tricks.

They rode long and hard. The watchtower appeared an hour or

so after their departure. A great wooden wall blocked all inward passage but the pines were tall enough to stretch above it. They crossed the distance in a short time and found a group of men sleeping around the coals of a dying campfire.

Hilda dismounted and kicked one of them so hard with her steel-toed boot that there was a crack. The man woke with a start.

He was blond-bearded, and, judging by the indignation on his face he was the captain. "How dare you, woman!" He clutched his shoulder.

"Shut up!" Hilda hissed. "Open the gate, or—by the Green Dragon's slippery scales—I will skin you alive and feed your innards to the darklings, just like you did to my friend."

"I am cousin to the earl!" he started.

"That's why he doesn't feed you to the darklings, I'd guess," Hilda sneered. She pressed the sword-blade up to his neck, easing off just enough so that it did not break skin. "And these men—I suppose the reason why they aren't fed to the darklings is so they could protect your cowardly hide. Or maybe these men are your lovers, and you're their blushing bride."

The captain's cheeks flashed red.

"Anger, or embarrassment that I told the truth? I can't tell," Hilda said. "But don't talk, Hargin. I know you, worm. You're the biggest coward in Badelgard, and if you do not march up to that gate and open it within the next three seconds, I swear I will cut off your head right now, because I am a smart woman and can figure out how to open a wooden gate—as can any of these men you whore yourself out to."

Brand laughed. He was beginning to respect Hilda.

Captain Hargin slowly stood to his feet, eyes filled with rage.

"Hands up!" Hilda snapped.

He obeyed.

"Brand, remove his sword."

Brand pulled the sword out of its hilt. It was a fine work of steel.

"That will be yours from now on, Brand," Hilda said. She

glanced at Hargin. "Open the gate, worm. Go on, or I will cut off the instrument of your whorishness."

Brand didn't know if egging Hargin on was a good strategy, but he laughed just the same. Happy to have a weapon, he followed Hilda as she forced Hargin toward the gate. The captain walked inside a small chamber just outside the gate and began cranking the thing open.

"Soon as he comes out," Hilda whispered, "I'll cut off his head."

"Leave him be," Brand said. "Leave him to his shame. It's better than needless killing. It'll prove you're right—he's the biggest coward in all Badelgard, and he won't be able to escape it."

Hilda smiled. "That is unwise. Yet if it is your wish, I will grant it."

Hargin cranked the gate open and they entered the Darkling Wood. The gate then began cranking shut.

"Now you'll die, woman!" Hargin shouted, laughing hysterically. "You'll die, and you'll eat your insults when the monsters come! They'll rip your arms off, dog! I watch them every day with pleasure. Your man is gone... gone! The darklings have already ripped him limb from limb!"

CHAPTER NINE

The Darkling Wood was silent, yet Brand could feel in his bones that it was not empty. There were things watching them.

"If we see a corpse, we must chop it into pieces," Hilda said. "The corpses move with the speed of a White Wolf."

Brand grasped his sword tightly. Gunnar had given him a little training, but not enough for him to bear a sword with anything approaching competence.

"Gunnar!" Hilda shouted. "Gunnar?"

There was a nonsensical whispering behind them, perhaps in a different language. Brand looked back. Standing a few yards away was a little girl, her head cocked at an impossible angle and dry blood covering her mouth. Her stomach was swollen. Hilda grabbed Brand's shoulder to restrain him.

"It's a darkling," she explained. "See that belly of hers? She is not pregnant; it's from eating human flesh."

Nausea seized Brand, but he held it in.

There was a harsh cracking noise as the little girl's head fell off and rolled onto the floor. As it rolled, the lips moved. "Your friend is one of us now."

Hilda charged at the little girl, heaved back her sword, and, in one hard slash, chopped her in two. Brand winced as she hacked off the hands, then the legs, and finally, the feet. Then she turned around. "Remember, she is not a girl. She is something entirely different."

"I know," Brand said quietly.

"Where is Gunnar?" Brand said as they walked through the silent forest.

"I know some things about this wood," Hilda answered him. "But, by far, not all of it. I have no idea where Gunnar might be."

From the darkness of the forest, a voice began humming the

tune of "Fell Winter"—the song the earl had liked and the one that Hilda despised. Brand froze in place. Hilda held her sword high.

"*And the Ulfr shall have their revenge,*" it sang, "*and the Ulfr shall have their revenge.*"

A figure in a dark, hooded cloak walked gracefully out of the forest. Green fingers drooped from the gold-rimmed sleeves. Behind the figure was an army of darkling corpses, and guarding the figure were two men, one blond-bearded and one brown-bearded, both rigidly frozen.

"Agni! Rannulf! My loves," Hilda cried. "What has this monster done to you?"

"Agni and Rannulf love their mother," a woman's voice said from behind the cowl. "As do all my children. You have hacked one to pieces; I shall put poor Asgerd back together in a short time. I am an expert seamstress, as all mothers should be. You, human girl. Do you seam? Surely you do—it is every human woman's duty!"

"Show your face, monster," Hilda hissed, "Or I shall cleave it from the neck and see it for myself."

"You're an Ulfr witch, aren't you?" Brand shouted, holding his sword out firmly but shakily. "What did you do with my lord, Gunnar? Speak!"

The witch laughed. "Your friend is my child, now."

"Liar!" Brand snapped.

"Don't you realize that, if I willed it, I could blacken your flesh and adopt you as my child?" The witch laughed. "And don't you realize that, without the aid of the Green Dragon, the humans of Badelgard have no way of stopping me? You humans foolishly kill your witch-children, and burn the wizards who come of age at the stake. Now, what sort of power do you have against us? How in the wide world can you protect yourself when my race returns? You had your three-hundred years of play and frolic; now it is time for me to reclaim what is justly mine."

"Vile witch!" Hilda snapped, but her shouting could not mask the trembling in her voice. "You Ulfr were the most perverted of all nations. Your brothers married your sisters... you sacrificed little children to your demon-goddess... you ate your dead even when the harvest was good! How could you ever claim justice?"

The witch laughed. "You're so simple, seeing things in two shades: black and white, good and evil. There is always gray... and colors—bright, beautiful colors—which you humans seem not to wear in your short, sad lives. But even so, there are no blacks, whites, grays, or colors when it comes to life; there is only strength and weakness, wisdom and stupidity."

"We crushed you in times past," Hilda shouted. "And by Vana, we'll crush you again!"

"Crush me?" the witch said. She extended her hands out of her sleeves. Her fingers were like green vines. A black light grew in her palms. "It is time to end this conversation; I've grown bored with your dumbness, girl."

Hilda gasped, as if she could not breathe, and stumbled. Her skin shimmered and then darkened. Brand screamed and began to charge, but it was no use; a White Wolf's piercing howl filled the forest like a shrieking winter wind. A pack of giant, snow-colored wolves sprinted up to the Ulfr witch and her darkling children. They growled.

"Dogs! Wolves!" the witch screamed. "The most unclean of beasts! I shall hunt every last one of you, and make stew out of your hearts."

One White Wolf dashed up to Brand and lay down on the floor, then barked. Not sure what to do, Brand sat down on his back, and then the White Wolf dashed off in the direction of the neighboring great peak. He looked back, and Hilda had followed. The gnawing, withering sounds of the Ulfr witch's dark spells filled the air as the rosy light of dawn slowly crept into the horizon and Brand and Hilda were borne away toward the mountains as if by a propitious wind.

CHAPTER TEN

The White Wolves carried Brand and Hilda high up the peak. As they leapt up rocky cliffs and ascended steep inclines, Brand occasionally thought of running away. The wolves could very well intend to eat them, but the way the wolf had beckoned Brand to sit on him indicated otherwise.

By the time they stopped their ascent, it was well into the morning. Exhaustion had begun to seep into Brand, and when the bumpy ride ended he nearly dozed off. The wolves walked through a veil of snowy black pines, and entered an ice cave. There, Brand hopped off his wolf and sat against the ice wall, shivering. The air was cold and dead.

A male wolf trotted up to him. He was the largest and most muscular of the lot. A scar ran across his blue eyes. Baring dark yellow fangs, the wolf reached out with his right paw and scratched hard into the ice with one of his claws.

"Don't eat me! Be a nice boy." Brand's voice cracked.

The wolf snarled and beat his paw onto the ice. Brand looked down at the scratchings the wolf had made.

"I don't know what you want!"

The wolf barked twice and hit the ice with both paws. Brand looked down once more. Only then did he realize that the wolf had scratched two crude runes into the ice. They were in old Badelgard script, but he had learned that language at the Skalds' College. They read, "Friend. Danger."

"Yes! Yes. I know, my friend is in danger," Brand said, baffled that these wolves were communicating. There had always been legends of White Wolves talking, but he always assumed they were just that: legends.

The wolf backed away and began scratching again. This time he wrote five runes. They read, "Great Need. Healing. Carry. Southward. To Gulls."

"Gulls?" Brand said, confused.

The wolf snarled.

Hilda spoke from across the room. "Andarr's Port has gulls in summer. Do you mean Andarr's Port, boy?"

The wolf snarled loudly and growled in a low tone as he approached Hilda. With great force he dug his claw into the ice and scratched three runes: "King."

"I apologize, your majesty," Hilda said. "You are a king, and a proud, noble beast."

The alpha wolf scratched more runes: "Danger. Coming. Take. Leave."

A she-wolf dragged the body of Gunnar across the ice. His legs were cut off just below the knees, his stumps somehow healed and not bleeding. His skin had darkened, and his eyes had yellowed.

Brand let out a scream that lasted several seconds. "Master! Master! Is he alive?"

"He's unconscious, but he's breathing, boy," Hilda said. "I'll carry him."

The alpha let out a wintry howl and all the wolves bolted out of the cave except the one who had dragged in Gunnar. She wrote the rune for "Follow."

Hilda carried Gunnar as she, Brand, and the White Wolf navigated down the eastern side of the slope. Their descent was far more awkward than the ascent; they could not manage the steep cliffs and rocks as well as the White Wolves, especially Hilda with Gunnar. The descent lasted until the sun was nearly in the middle of the sky.

They reached the bottom, and, despite their exhaustion, continued through the black pines. Eventually they came to the wooden wall. They were on the other side—the safe side that faced White Wolf Keep. Brand ran his hands along the coarse wood and thanked Vana that the Ulfr had not taken them.

The White Wolf scratched more runes into the dirt: "Carry. Holy Place. Gulls. Before Dusk." Then she howled and took off, bounding up toward the mountains, toward the place she came from.

Brand needed sleep. Even now, his eyelids were drooping shut. But he trusted these White Wolves. Andarr's Port was sixteen miles southwest down through the plains and down a sharp descent to the seashore. That was a long journey, even for someone who hadn't slept all night. And now that late morning had arrived, there was very little chance they could get there before dusk.

Hilda screamed in frustration. "This man is heavy as a boulder! Why, gods? Why?"

Then Midnight came galloping in from the north, whinnying as the first snow of the winter began drifting down from the silver sky.

CHAPTER ELEVEN

Even if Gunnar had not been unconscious, riding three-a-saddle on Midnight would be impossible. So Hilda fixed him to the saddle and, despite their exhaustion, they half-walked, half-ran, down the southwest-leading trail as fast as they could as the snow fell.

They reached White Wolf Keep in the afternoon, but made a point to avoid it; they were fugitives now—both in Frostfall and Ostergard—and whether the city of Andarr's Port would look the other way was any man's guess. But beyond doubt, they knew Lord Henrik would not look past it.

The snow piled up throughout the day as they hurried down the path. Soon it was up to Brand's heels. The road seemed to go on and on with no hint of termination. No signposts led the way. Over time, the sun descended in the sky, unnoticeably but inevitably.

The ground was truly dropping below them, now, in a steep, rocky descent. This almost-vertical drop continued for a quarter of an hour, and then a great river appeared below them. They were in the lowlands.

They followed the river west as the sun set in bronze colors. They came to a crossroads. A signpost read, "Andarr's Port: four miles." The sun was dipping below the now-visible sea as the rocky slopes of the river valley widened into flat, sandy land.

The winds picked up. The snow had deepened to Brand's thigh and Hilda's calf. Midnight began to whinny and neigh and toss her head about, and despite Hilda's reassurances the mare kept up her nervous demeanor.

The lights of a great city, built on either side of the river, appeared before them. Blocking view of anything but the rooftops was a tall stone wall. In time they reached a great wooden gate. A watchman stood on top of the battlements with a bow in his hands.

"Who are you?" he shouted. "The honorable Lord Harald has no desire whatsoever to harbor the unwanted, sickly, or poor. And if you come from any other keep having a price on your head, be aware that your punishment will be ten times worse here."

"Milord!" Hilda shouted. "We are not unwanted, nor are we sickly or poor. Nor do we bear a penalty on our heads of any kind."

Despite his sleepiness, Brand smiled wearily; not a single thing Hilda had just said was true.

"Are you a widow?" the watchman asked. "We are not a safe harbor for widows either."

"I am not a widow. This man here—" she said, and touched Brand's hand, "is my loving husband."

Brand gulped.

"An unlikely pairing. And who is that legless man in the saddle?"

"This," Hilda said, "This is my friend."

"What do you have to offer Andarr's Port?"

Hilda cast a worried glance into the creeping darkness.

"I have my lute," Brand said. "I am trained by the Skalds' College. I can play every instrument known in Badelgard, and I know as many songs as I've heard."

"I'll let you in," the watchman grunted. "Go to the Sunset Inn on the bay and tell the innkeeper I sent you. Name of Ivan. Nice man, and he's looking for a singer. He has the best spiced lamb in all Badelgard... actually, the only spiced lamb, far as I know." He glanced at Hilda. "And what about you? What talents do you possess?"

"I will not go in without my... dear wife," Brand said, glancing furtively at Hilda.

"I suppose the legless oaf comes in too," the watchman said. "Very well."

Andarr's Port was the largest town Brand had ever seen. The thatch-roofed, sturdily-built homes were crammed together, blocking out most sight of the quiet rock-walled bay. It was larger than Oskir, even though Brand—an easterner—knew that Andarr's Port had no army of its own; the High King was responsible for its defense. It was the only port into Badelgard. Spices, incense, strange animals, and foreign gold made its way into the port's marketplace, and because of its wealth, it was necessary to make it dependent on the High King.

On the way to the bay, they passed three brothels—the Cathouse, the Pleasure Palace, and the Lion's Den—all advertised with graphic pictures of nude women. There was only one brothel in Oskir, and, if they were not illegal there, they had been absent in White Wolf Keep.

Along the seashore, elevated high above the buildings was a stone castle with a green garden. Hilda pointed to it and said, "That's Riverhall Keep, built more for pleasure than defense."

"Who lives there?" Brand asked.

"Harald Riverhall, Baron of Andarr's Port. The king does not grant him the title of 'earl' because he fears it will make him ambitious. But from what I've heard, Harald is the least ambitious man in Badelgard."

"Have you been here before?" Brand said.

"When I left the horse chiefs, I came here and stayed a few months. I soon grew tired of these people's soft ways, their luxury and unwillingness to take up swords," Hilda said. "And the House Riverhall—what is supposed to a noble warrior house—is the worst of the lot. They are the most luxuriant, decadent vermin on the face of the earth." She paused and then felt Gunnar's cheek with the back of her hand. "Now we have to get this man some rest. Let's take him to the Sunset Inn and set him in a nice bed."

"The White Wolf said to take him to a holy place," Brand said.

"A night's rest in bed can do much more than any valkyrie or goddess can," Hilda said. "I take that back; it will do much more."

"I disagree. I think—"

"Don't think, boy," Hilda said. "How long have you been on this earth?"

"Well… I have lived through twenty-six winters."

"This winter will be my fortieth," Hilda said. "I've survived longer than anyone I knew as a child, and I will survive for many more years. Valkyries and goddesses did nothing for me. Only my own strength and resourcefulness did."

Brand said nothing. He obeyed, and realized that this woman had subdued him more than Gunnar ever had. He supposed that Hilda had been through more than Gunnar, and in spite of the pressures men forced upon her as a woman. She had survived to a ripe age, and Brand had not yet.

They got to the inn. Hilda had a little coin from her thieving adventures, enough for two nights at the inn. After that, their plans were uncertain. They carried Gunnar into their room and set him on the bed, wrapping him in warm sheets. They'd need to get him some nourishment.

In their private chamber, Brand dripped the mead down Gunnar's throat little by little. He hummed to his master to calm his nerves. Then, as he swallowed the last bit of mead, Gunnar gasped and spoke.

"I have seen the Great Witch. I have seen her unmasked, beneath her cloak," he rasped, eyes closed. "She is cold as a winter rain… graceful as a queen… blue-eyed, fair-haired… beautiful as death." He paused for a second. "Her children have eaten my legs… the wolves took me away, but I don't want to stray from my mother. I don't want to go away from her."

"Master!" Brand said. "She isn't your mother. She's an evil Ulfr."

Gunnar gasped for air again. "The shadow is growing on me. I can see the twilit sky… night is coming for me… she will take me."

"I won't let her take you!" Brand snapped.

Hilda looked at Brand sternly. "Don't shout."

Gunnar reached toward the ceiling. "The shadow is falling over me, Brand… there isn't hope for me."

"No!" Brand said. "There is hope for you." He shook Gunnar. "Wake up." He opened his eyelids in an attempt to startle him. The pupils were now dark red and the whites, silver. They stared into space, seeing yet not seeing.

"It will be too late for me soon, Brand," Gunnar wheezed. "It will be too late. I will join the darklings."

Hilda stood up from her bed, a grave expression on her face. She laid her fingers round the hilt of her sword. "We must kill him."

"No!" Brand said.

Hilda looked at Brand sternly. "It would be merciful to kill him now. The witch has claimed him. If we do not kill him, we will be making a horrid mistake; he will arise as part of her evil, as one of her children. He will not be Gunnar; he will be the witch's servant."

"I won't let you!" Brand said. "I've let you tell me what to do for most of my journey, woman, but—"

Hilda drew her sword an inch out of the scabbard. "What does my womanhood have to do with anything?" she said. "Troll-Cutter has drunk the blood of many men. It has slain earls' men, bandit chiefs, boy-children, and singing dandies." She paused. "So listen to me, boy. If we do not kill Gunnar, he will kill us. That fact does not change if the one who told you is a woman."

Brand said nothing. His eyes watered as he realized Hilda was right.

Hilda glanced at him, seeing this affirmation, then eyed her sword. "Take him outside. There is a public garden where only criminals and fools walk at night. We will dispatch him there."

"I will not watch."

Brand awoke in tears. Hilda had told him that the death was painless. He had sobbed late into the night. Soon the pillow grew wet, and his eyes had dried up. A gaping emptiness filled him; he would not be able to sing tonight, nor play his lute. He had been through seven winters with Gunnar. He had been the man's skald; and now he was dead. He would compose a song to honor him, but not today. Today, he would only mourn.

Hilda sat across from him on another bed. She was frowning and empathy touched her double-scarred face. "I am sorry, Brand," she said softly. "I can only imagine your pain. And I'm sorry for calling you a dandy and a child." She moved over to Brand's bed and laid a hand around his shoulder, then hugged him tight. "I will never replace him for you. But I will do my best to ease your pain. I can go get you some fresh food from the market. There is pickled herring, salmon and lobster… sweet cakes, honey loaves… tea… anything you can imagine, the market has it."

"No," Brand said. His face was raw and dry. "I'll go with you."

Outside, the bright clothing of the populace blinded Brand. Even in Oskir, the citizens wore dull reds and blues at their finest. The people of the port wore reds as luminous as rubies, greens colorful as summer grass, and oranges bright as flame. In the sunlight, Brand noticed that even the houses and shops of Andarr's Port were painted in pastel yellows, greens and blues, so totally unlike the grayness of White Wolf Keep or Oskir.

Yet even this visual feast could not distract him from Gunnar. He had been a good man. A great friend. And the Ulfr witch had claimed him.

Nor did what he came next help him any more: just outside the marketplace, a dozen men and women sat in chairs and watched a tied-up man on a chopping block. An executioner dressed in black stood there with a headsman's sword, and a judge stood behind a lectern as he read from a slip of parchment.

"Ingald son of Ingvald, chicken thief, is hereby sentenced to die by command of the honorable Lord Harald Riverhall."

"Shield your eyes, boy," Hilda whispered.

Brand hesitated and saw it all. The executioner slashed down hard and broke part way through Ivan's neck. Blood exploded from the wound. Only after another hard slash did the bloody head fly off the neck and roll onto the ground. The viewers cheered.

"A morbid entertainment," Brand mused.

"Aye," answered Hilda. "And if death is the punishment for chicken thieves, what would the punishment be for something more severe?"

They exchanged glances and there was nervousness in her eyes.

The marketplace had spice stalls, beer kegs, wine bottles, and exotic animals from the south; elven jewelry, elven knives, and costly reams of spidersilk from the north; scented woods and moose antlers from the west; and things Brand had never seen before.

Nailed to a large wooden post in the center of the market was the Hangman's List, recently updated. Brand strayed from Hilda—who was looking at the elven knives longingly—and gave it a careful look. At the bottom, he found his name:

BRAND, SON OF GUTLAFF (CRIME: BREAKING THE KING'S SEAL. PRESCRIBED PUNISHMENT: TORTURE, FOLLOWED BY BEHEADING.)

GUNNAR WHORESON, BASTARD OF MAGNUS BLACKHELM (CRIME: BREAKING THE KING'S SEAL. PRESCRIBED PUNISHMENT: TORTURE, FOLLOWED BY BEHEADING.)

He searched and found Hilda's name further up:

HILDA SUMMERLEAF (CRIME: FLEEING THE EARL'S SERVICE ‹TWO COUNTS›. MURDER ‹NINE COUNTS›. THEFT ‹TEN COUNTS›. LYING TO AN EARL ‹FIVE COUNTS›. CROSS-DRESSING ‹TWO COUNTS.› PRESCRIBED PUNISHMENT: BEHEADING.)

Hilda was of a noble house; Brand knew this, but the listing brought it to the fore of his mind. Brand could not say the same; nor could Gunnar—gods rest his soul. As a member of a warrior house, Hilda would not be tortured even as a murderess and thief. Though Hilda had gone against her father's wishes, and fled her execution—not to mention her other crimes—she would always be of noble warrior blood and torture, for her, would remain unthinkable. Brand, the son of a swineherd—though given musical talent by the goodness of Vana— would always be a swineherd's son.

"Better not stare at that too long," Hilda said from behind him. "People will get suspicious."

Brand turned around. He regarded Hilda coldly, that undeservedly lucky woman. What did it matter that Brand's father took care of pigs, and Hilda's father was the patriarch of some unimportant noble house?

Bells rang from the High Temple of Vana—death bells, mourning bells. The people in the marketplace looked around in confusion. There were two loud trumpet peals, and then a group of horsemen in purple, gold-threaded robes shoved their way through the market crowd and up to the high central lectern.

Brand followed Hilda to the lectern, gazing at her long blonde hair and her fair neck with anger. She had killed Gunnar. He had let her do it. Gunnar, his only friend in a dark world that had no respect for swineherds' sons, was dead. And that woman—that vile, joyless, noble woman—had done the deed.

A man walked up onto the lectern. A golden coronet rested on his short black hair. His face was handsome and his beard was thinly trimmed. This had to be Harald, scion of the House of Riverhall. Judging by the coronet, it could only be Harald. It could only be the baron: the hedonist, the connoisseur—no, the glutton—of whores, and frequenter of brothels. Soft, luxuriant, Hilda had called him.

Better than a joyless thief.

When the crowd was gathered at the lectern, he spoke. "The High King is dead." There were a few cheers, but they died down after Harald's expression turned stern. "Sven's only surviving son, Osvald, is not yet of age. In the interim, Lord Sigmund Blackhelm, eldest son of Magnus Blackhelm, has assumed the High Throne at Oskir."

"Boo!" someone cried.

"As baron of Andarr's Port, I honor this change of leadership. Life will continue on as it always has," said Harald. "I will serve King Sigmund as his loyal subject until Osvald Oster comes of age."

King Sven had been healthy when Brand and Gunnar left him, as he had been throughout his reign. The only thing different was the Idol of the Great Mother they had given him.

Brand's stomach turned.

"There is one more bit of news I must share with you," Harald shouted. "Tonight, I hear there will be a powerful storm. There are dark clouds forming over the sea and the air is changed. Stay inside and near the fire." He looked around and opened his mouth, as if hesitating. "That is all," he finally said, and then abruptly stepped down from the lectern and left with his purple-garbed retinue.

Hilda turned around to face Brand. "He didn't want to tell us about the darklings... they've spread south. Ol' Harald didn't want to rile them up or tell them that his guard post outside the city was savaged by the darklings and now there is blood everywhere. Typical Riverhall behavior! Always wanting to be popular and well-liked, never wanting to bear bad news."

"You certainly learn things fast."

"I've made many friends over my career. And those friends have many friends of their own." Hilda smiled. "My friend Sigvar tells me the darklings slew a tributary in Riverhall Forest, a mile outside the city. Said it was carrying a tribute of gold to the Dragonmount Temple; they never use the main roads for tributaries. Thirty heavily armed, heavily armored soldiers clawed, gutted, and torn to shreds by darklings. Looks like the men exploded, Sigvar says. We better hurry; some others have caught wind of it."

"The darklings don't come out by day, I suppose," Brand said quietly, still thinking of Gunnar. "We still have a few hours ere nightfall."

He would prove himself as strong as her.

CHAPTER TWELVE

Thick snowflakes began to fall when they reached Riverhall Forest. Some leaves still clung to the thin white aspens, but most had been shed for the winter. Now, a carpet of gold lay over the forest. This wood—a place of meditation for the noble line, as Hilda explained—grew a quarter mile north of the main road.

Inside the wood were marble statues faded gray by the rain, snow, and wind. There was a statue of a woman just inside the wood: "Astrid Riverhall, Mother of Our Line," an inscription read. In her stone hands she clasped a bowl filled to the brim with water.

Brand shrugged off a spear of envy at these people's enchanted lives, though now they were long dead.

They found the wrecked caravan minutes later; Riverhall Forest was small. Blood, guts, and severed limbs filled the ground surrounding a small wagon. Yet they were not alone. A young man stood beside it, scooping gold coins from a cracked-open chest into a burlap sack. A short scabbard hung from his belt.

Brand would prove himself brave. "Stop right there!" he shouted, and drew the sword he stole from Hargin. "That's our gold."

The man turned around, and he drew his sword. He was young, perhaps sixteen or seventeen, and had dark whiskers—no beard yet. He had the aquiline nose, the high cheekbones, and the dark hair of Harald Riverhall, but was not Harald. "Is it your gold?" he sneered. "I thought these were a portion of the year's taxes, being sent as aid to the Dragonpriest, sacred of our lord Skruga."

Brand realized two things; firstly, he had made a very poor choice, and, secondly, there was no chance at all that he could defeat this man.

"Tell me, commoner scum, if you realize who you speak to."

Brand said nothing.

"I am Stenn Riverhall, first in line to the barony, and I will kill you if you take a step closer, you worthless, common-as-dirt vermin."

"Don't talk to him like that!" snapped Hilda. "I may be a woman, but if you continue, I will be your end."

Stenn howled with laughter. "A woman—a common woman—thinks she can defeat me?"

"I am no common woman," Hilda said. "I am of the line of Summerleaf, and I consider this man, Brand, as my equal."

"The Summerleafs are a laughing stock. Piss-poor, and own about as much land as a commoner. Skotja Village, that's it. Ha!" Stenn grinned. "And if you're Hilda Summerleaf, you've earned yourself quite a notorious spot on the Hangman's List. I will be proud to be the one who caught the rat."

"I, Hilda of the House Summerleaf, challenge you, Stenn of the House Riverhall, to a duel," Hilda said.

Stenn's mocking demeanor turned to a solemn stare. "I accept your challenge, as befits my honor, but I shall set the terms," he said. "We duel to first blood. If I win, you will come back with me to Riverhall Keep to answer to my uncle Harald. You will also be my slave. And your friend will die."

Brand gulped.

"And if I win," Hilda said, "then you will absolve both me and my friend of my crimes, and give us safe haven in Andarr's Port."

Stenn was silent for a while, apparently poring over the terms. Finally, he said, "Your demands are steep, but I accept, Hilda Summerleaf." Then he drew his sword out of its scabbard: a small weapon. Circular, abstract patterns ran along the leaf-shaped blade, and gems were inset periodically along the inner groove. It was an elven sword, light yet strong, which only the fantastically wealthy could afford and which Hilda could only ever gawk at in the marketplace.

Hilda drew her own weapon, a bulky head-cleaver of a sword. Brand took a step forward with his own sword, but Hilda looked back at him and glanced at him sternly. "Stay out of this, Brand. I must duel with honor," she said.

I used to be idealistic, like you. I used to believe in honor. Those were

Hilda's own words back at White Wolf Keep. Brand stood back, trembling slightly, watching the fight begin in the golden wood.

Brand looked on as Stenn struck fast with his elven blade and Hilda just barely blocked with her unwieldy weapon. Hilda swept her sword in a hard cross-cut, but Stenn ducked and the blade swooped over his head. Stenn barreled forward and thrust at her with his own blade, and Hilda dodged out of the way, bringing her sword crashing down in a near miss. Then Stenn twirled around and cut hard, slicing through Hilda's jerkin. Brand winced as blood began trickling down.

Hilda felt the wound, then knelt in front of him. Stenn laid the flat of his blade on her shoulder. "You were foolish to challenge me," Stenn said. "I have been trained by elven swordmasters of the north. I am a master of the Viper and Pincer Crab Forms... and you... you fight like a dying bear."

"You have a weapon of light metal and can wave it like a feather—a weapon I could never afford. The cleavers of the northmen are not meant for dueling," Hilda said, "but I take responsibility for my choice. I was overbold."

"Don't make excuses, or I will kill you now rather than give you my uncle's justice." He turned to Brand. "And you. You are common, correct? Not even a piss-poor Summerleaf, are you? Common as dirt?"

A trembling seized Brand. His stomach turned and he felt the need to relieve himself. Yet he felt himself unable to flee; he was frozen in place.

"I'm sure the people will have fun seeing you tortured," Stenn said. "The people like to see criminals get their justice."

"My lord," Hilda said, "if your honor would lend me ear, I must say that this man possesses a skill that would be of use to you. I beg of you, do not kill him; it would be like throwing away that pile of gold."

"A skill?" Stenn asked. "What sort of skill?"

"He is trained by the Skalds' College in Oskir," Hilda said. "He is the best singer and lutist I have ever heard. He knows songs of joy and mirth that will get you through the worst of winter."

"Joy? Mirth?" Stenn scoffed. "I prefer songs that frighten me and make my little sister weep: songs of darkness and endless winters… of rokahn, and giants, and spiders big as dogs… and the Ulfr of old."

"I know many of those songs," Brand said, his voice still trembling. "If it is darkness you want, I can fill all your idle hours."

"We take him to a holding cell, and if his songs please me, I will let him live for a while until he outgrows his usefulness." Stenn looked down at Hilda. "And if you are a competent assassin, as your crimes suggest, then I believe you won't outgrow your own use for a while. I'll keep you alive until my uncle Harald forces your execution."

CHAPTER THIRTEEN

By the time they reached Riverhall Keep, the snow flurries blinded them. Icy winds knifed through the air, burning through their fur coats with deadening cold. The sun was now a twinkling, fading glow against the sea and darkness was fast approaching. The darklings would soon fill the countryside, or perhaps now that they'd had their fill, would retreat back past the wooden wall—Brand could only hope.

They reached the gate of the keep. The guards were dressed in gold-colored armor, and had on linen overshirts bearing the Riverhall coat-of-arms: the golden image of a bear with his feet on either side of a river, set against a blue field.

"These two are my prisoners," explained young Stenn. "Take them to the holding cells. Give them a little bit of slop, but not enough to spoil them."

The guards silently nodded affirmation. They took Brand and Hilda's swords from Stenn, then restrained them and led them into the fine stone rooms of Riverhall Keep.

The first thing Brand noticed was the temperature. The keep was well-heated and far more comfortable than White Wolf Keep. Only in King Sven's royal palace did Brand remember being this comfortable, and that was earlier in the year when the winter had not yet begun.

On the way to the prison he could not help but notice the riches inside: golden urns, marble statues covered in ornate jewelry, and paintings with such rich colors they seemed to glow in the torchlight. The smell of roast boar tantalized Brand's stomach, making him realize just how hungry he was.

The moment they entered the prison wing, everything changed. The fine stone turned rough-hewn and the tile floors became flagstone. A large dog with torn-up ears greeted them with a snarl. In the whole of the prison, there was only one torch, and the cells which Brand and Hilda were thrown into—although close to each other—were nearly pitch black.

The guards left. A few seconds later, a pale, fat-bellied man dressed in black arrived. He grinned, revealing the few yellow teeth he had, and said, "I'll have your slop in a second. It's wha' the pigs eat down in the sty, but you can't afford to be picky when you're under my care."

After one bite of the slop—a crude, pummeled-down mixture of every undesirable food-scrap the court threw away, from fat to guts and gizzards—Brand decided that starving was better than finishing his meal. Across the room, through iron bars, he could see that Hilda had finished hers. Their eyes met and she laughed.

"When you've been starving in the mossland and you've forced down raw squirrel guts without spewing them back out, you can eat anything," Hilda said.

Brand stared at her in disbelief, and then they both burst out laughing, howling like wolves. Brand's laughter turned to tears, and soon his face was red and wet. "It is nice to have a laugh during such a dark time… when my master is dead, and there is no food to warm my gullet… and I will be tortured in public for entertainment, then a sword finally thrust through my neck." Brand's tears turned back into laughter, and then a mixture of both. For a while it exorcised his fear and sadness. He wished he and Hilda shared a cell. He looked at her and realized her strength had made her pretty to him, despite her scars and age; she was more beautiful to him a young maiden. "If you were near to me, Hilda, I'd kiss you," he said out loud. "I'd kiss you until you couldn't breathe and your lips turned raw."

"I am old," Hilda said. "Old in body, but older in the soul; I would not let you kiss me. My childbearing years are near over and you are in the prime of life. I am old enough to be your mother. You deserve a beautiful lady young as yourself, healthy and scarce of years."

"I'd kiss you just the same."

The jailer shouted from the darkness. "I'll make you both kiss my rump if you don't shut up!"

Despite the crude retort, a lust for Hilda had flared up inside him. He had not been with a woman in a long, long time, and those two scars from the crude horse chieftain were more beautiful to him than a noblewoman's fine white powder. Only now, separated by iron bars, did his feelings show. He laughed.

Hours passed in silence. Outside, the winds began howling, audible even through the thick stone. The cells grew chill, even in the well-heated keep. And the jailer came in and unlocked Brand's door, but not Hilda's. "The court wishes to see you," he grunted.

Brand gave a passing glance to Hilda inside her cell. Then he left with the jailer.

The whole Riverhall family sat inside the court room. The floors were covered in bearskins and deerskins, and strange orange-and-black skins which Brand had never seen before. The windows were draped with purple silk. Colored paper lined the walls; gold leaf lined the window ledges; and every cup, bowl and utensil which the family used to eat was made of silver. The ostentatious display made Brand hate these people all the more.

Sitting on the throne was Harald, a coronet resting on his thin black hair. Sable lined the sleeves of his thick winter robe. Next to him was his wife, a blonde woman with her hair done into a bun.

Harald's relatives sat around him on couches and the fur-cushioned floor. There were, perhaps, five children in his dark brood: Stenn, the only boy; and four little girls in dresses. There was one other older adult, not counting Harald and his wife: a woman with brown hair and blue eyes.

All their features were dark save Harald's blonde wife. Perhaps these children belonged to Harald's brother, as Stenn did. But Harald's brother was not present.

"Greetings," said Lord Harald. "My nephew says you are a skald, and trained at the Skalds' College."

"He does not lie," Brand answered.

"I am a lover of music," Harald said. "But first… you were caught trespassing in my wood. What were you doing there?"

I used to be idealistic, like you. I used to believe in honor.

"Going for a walk," Brand lied.

"I know you are not telling the truth," said Lord Harald. "It does not matter to me. What matters to me is that you can sing; I shall not put a musical talent to waste."

"If you kill my friend, Hilda," Brand said, "then I will not sing for you."

"Then you will die!" Stenn snapped.

Harald motioned him to be silent. "We will keep her alive, then," he said. "Do not listen to my nephew. He loves to see violence; he's acquired the tastes of the portsmen. An earl's first job is to be liked. If the people want to see executions, they will see it. And believe me, they want to." He paused. "Now, skald, please sing me a song."

"What kind would you like?"

Stenn interrupted. "Winter! Spiders! Rokahn and giants!"

Stenn's mother—the brunette—glared at her son.

"My tastes stray to the dark as well," said Lord Harald. "Please me, and I will let you have some boar and mead."

Brand gave his lute a few test strums. Then, swallowing his nervousness, he began playing the opening to Fell Winter and sang as best he could in the circumstances.

Men will abandon honor
Kin will turn against kin
Snow-age, dark-age, White Wolf-age
'til the Ulfr have their revenge
'til the Ulfr have their revenge

As he sang the last bit, young Stenn jumped about and clapped excitedly. "That was amazing!" he said. "Sing me one about trolls!"

The brown-haired woman—Stenn's mother—frowned. "Calm down, Stenn," she said. "This music is frightening Unna." She clutched tight a little girl in pigtails who was obviously not frightened, then glared at Brand.

"Quiet, Lady Kenna. It is good to be scared on a cold winter's night," Harald said. "You have a good ear, and your voice is pleasing. Yet I do believe you need work."

Brand was too worried about his safety to be insulted.

"I do think you can become a great skald, however," Harald said. "And you may have a helping of boar and a stein of mead. Your friend, however, is a wanted criminal. You only broke the king's seal and fled the earl's service; she is a murderess, a thief, and more. She once whored herself to an earl's man in Blackhelm Keep, then cut his throat and left with his coinpurse. She is dangerous and must be stopped. If I abided her here in this city I would be a terrible baron."

"She is misunderstood!" Brand asserted. "A horse chief—one of the horse peoples—she was sent to him by her father, and she was raped."

"Lord Dagnir Goldleaf is an ambitious man. He is sixty years old, and yet still devises ways to expand his house. His holdings are still small, his coffers still empty. Wise men have said, 'The goal of a noble house is to bring all others under its submission.' But I say bullocks." Harald motioned to his family. "Neither I, nor the House Riverhall, wish to go war. We only wish to live, and live well."

"And live well you do," Brand said. "You have an excellent keep, excellent food, and an excellent city."

"And yet, I do not live as well as I want," Harald said and glanced out the window, his eyes filled with thought. He glanced back at Brand. "I am not a bad man. Some may say I am a coward, but I only want the people to like me. I want you to like me, Brand. I will not kill Hilda straightaway, though I regret that I must, and soon."

That night, sleeping in his private room, he thought of Hilda and prayed to Vana that she might be saved.

CHAPTER FOURTEEN

He awoke in the middle of the night. Gunnar stood in the room, his chopped-up body crudely stitched back together, his axe in hand. His skin was silvery and the pupils of his eyes, dark red. "Why did you let her do that to me?" he said, his voice static and lifeless. "Why did you let her drag me out while I was still alive... struggling against her... taking me to the city park and then chopping off my legs and arms and hands and head? Why did you do that, my friend?"

Brand shrieked. "I am sorry, master. I thought the darklings took you. I thought they turned you into one of them. I thought—"

"Skalds," Gunnar said. "Always thinking... always thinking of things other than their master, wi' their heads in the clouds. Perhaps I'll do to you what they did to me... chop up the legs, then the arms, and the hands, an' save the head for last. Just like Hilda did to me, that dark-hearted wench."

He kept walking closer to Brand, and Brand kept backing away, but he'd hit the wall soon. In a black cookpot, above the dying coals of the fire, was a knife. He grabbed the hilt and pulled it out against Gunnar.

"Would you kill your master, boy?" Gunnar said. "Would you cut out 'is heart. I thought the bond between warrior and skald went beyond death. I thought our loyalty was paramount and true."

"You are not Gunnar!" Brand said. "You are one of the darklings! The dead who walk again. Your eyes are not the same... your skin is silver and strange."

"If you do not believe me," Gunnar said, "I'll kill you, an' I'll cut you up."

Brand charged him, surprising him, and knocked him down to the floor. He ran the knife hard against Gunnar's throat. He sawed it down to the spinal bone. Gunnar's body crumpled inward, then turned to gray powder, and then to nothing.

Brand awoke at first light. Sweat covered him, dripping down his neck and his arms and moistening his undershirt and tunic. The dream hung heavy over him. Or had it been a dream?

Two cooks were re-lighting the fireplace, evidently to cook the lord's breakfast.

Brand shivered, thinking of that dream, and felt a mix of guilt and fear. "What are we having for breakfast?" he asked, more to get his mind off things than actual concern.

"Spicy beef and leek stew," a cook said.

"May I give some to Hilda?"

"I suppose," the other said, "if the lord baron agrees."

Harald granted Brand's request when he awoke.

Brand took Hilda the steaming hot bowl before he had even tasted his own. He pushed it through the openings of the iron bars.

"Thank you," she said. "You are a good man. Any woman would be lucky to have you. But I am not that woman."

"I want you, Hilda," Brand said.

Hilda picked a wedge of beef out of the stew and chewed it down. She winced. "Have you had spice before? Has the hot pepper of the southerly peoples ever touched your tongue?"

"No," Brand said.

"You will not like it at first," Hilda said. "But the more you have it, the more you will enjoy it until you are like one of the southerners."

"I will never be like the southerners—the soft, cowardly people in their luxurious cities, knowing nothing of honor."

"Of all the towns in Badelgard, Andarr's Port is the most southerly in culture," Hilda said. "And of all the noble houses, the Riverhalls are the most southern and decadent. Remember this when you are their pet, and I am in chains."

There was a hint of accusation and bitterness toward Brand in Hilda's voice, and it tore at his heart.

Back in the throne room, the morning's breakfast had just begun—and Brand's tongue, just starting to burn from the spicy stew—when a man in a gray kirtle entered the hall.

"What is it, Eileff?" Harald said. "Couldn't this have waited until after breakfast?"

"I'm afraid not, Your Honor," he answered. "A horse has died in your stables… Silver, Lord Stenn's stallion."

"You sad excuse for an equerry!" Stenn screamed. "I'll have you hanged, you whore's son! I loved that stallion like a child."

"What happened?" Harald said in a tone no less biting than his nephew. "Silver was healthy. Why did you let him die?"

Eileff's face had grown pale. "I found him dead in the stables. I believe he died of terror."

"How do you know that?" Harald said.

"It pains me to admit this," said Eileff. "The horses went wild last night. Two managed to kick down their doors and escape." He gulped. "Including your palfrey Thunderhoof, milord, and Lady Kenna's gelding."

"You bastard," Lady Kenna hissed.

"Those were priceless easterly horses. We took great joy in riding them!" Harald shouted. "Where were you when all this happened?"

"I was in my house with a locked door," Eileff said. "I was hiding from the strangers who came to the city last night. The ghosts…"

Brand admired Eileff's bravery and truthfulness. He was an honorable man.

"Ghosts," Harald said, and then laughed. "And now poor Silver is dead, and Thunderhoof is gone… all because my equerry was afraid of ghosts! Have you no shame? I once thought you were a brave man… but now you hid from ghosts and abandoned your post." He jabbed a finger at Eileff. "Take him away. Off with his head, and give the people a good show."

Ten gold-armored guards protected the throne. The two by

Harald's side grabbed Eileff with their gloved hands.

"Promote Ennar, and scour the port for another junior equerry," said Harald.

Eileff went along with the guards without a struggle. Sickness settled in Brand's stomach as he realized just how easily he could share the equerry's fate.

An hour after Eileff was dragged off to his fate—and long after Brand had finished his tongue-burning stew—another man entered. He wore the gold armor of Harald's personal guardians and an overshirt bearing the Riverhall coat-of-arms.

"Lord Erik, Captain of the River Guard," Harald intoned darkly. "Why must you bother me? Have I not fed the people their daily allotment of execution? Did Eileff not please them? If not, go find someone who stared improperly at a market stall."

"Milord," the watch captain said, and dropped to one knee. "Jannik son of Jannik, Protector of the Watchtower and court favorite of the Frostfall earl, has a request."

Gooseflesh spread across Brand's skin. He thought of running away.

"He has no family name. So he is common," Harald said.

"He is a favorite of the earl," the watch captain said.

"Very well. Speak," Harald said.

"Jannik son of Jannik wants the woman, Hilda Summerleaf, whom we have in our custody. He wants her either as a prisoner, or as a severed head."

"No!" Brand shouted.

Harald glanced at Brand. "Why does he want her?" he said, looking back at the watch captain. "How has she wronged Jannik?"

"He has made claims of treason, and of endangering the people of Badelgard," said the watch captain.

"And if I refuse?" Harald said.

"Henrik, earl of White Wolf Keep, will come with an army and take her by force," the watch captain explained.

"Perhaps," said the blonde-haired queenly wife that sat next to Harald, "we should be brave, just this once. This woman is a dear friend of our beloved musician." She smiled at Brand. "If Henrik comes, the High King will defend us with an army far greater than the earl's. We are dependent to the king; but our jurisdiction over the port is close to sovereign."

Harald scratched his thin black beard in thought. "I will compromise. We will send her to this Jannik son of Jannik," he said. "And for the skald's sake, we will send her alive."

Better to send her beheaded; they would torture her and then hang her publicly in that barbaric keep.

"I do not wish our house to be cowardly," said Harald's wife. "But my husband is Lord Baron, and I am beholden to his commands. I am sorry, dear skald. Your music has made our lives so bright, and our evenings so pleasant; yet my husband cannot find it in his heart to properly repay you."

Harald's face was expressionless despite the accusation.

"It is decided, then," the watch captain said. "There is one other bit of rumor—that the Ulfr have returned."

"Don't tell the people such a fanciful story," Harald said. "It will frighten them and they will blame me."

As the watch captain turned to leave, Brand fell to his knees and folded his hands. "Please," he said, "let me see Hilda before she goes. I must say goodbye."

"That I will grant," Harald said.

They hauled Hilda out into the court, her hands bound in rope. She spat on the tile floor. "You are a dishonorable lout, Harald!" she hissed. "You send me off to my death while you sit on your cushioned throne. I am of a noble house and deserve better."

"You are a thief and a murderess," Harald said calmly.

"And you are not a man!" Hilda struggled against her rope but the guards jerked her into submission. "And you, Brand? Will you come with me?"

I used to be idealistic, like you. I used to believe in honor.

"No," Brand answered. "I tried to give you freedom. I failed. But I will give you this." He moved over and tried to kiss her.

Hilda shook away from him. "I don't want your kisses," she said. "You have no honor, boy."

"That is what you taught me," Brand said. "And I'm sorry for it all."

"Stuff your apologies," Hilda said. She looked up at the lord baron on his throne. "Enjoy your whores today, Harald!"

A flash of red touched Harald's cheeks. "Give her fifteen lashes before you take her!" he growled. "Let the people watch."

CHAPTER FIFTEEN

Soon after the incident, Brand retreated to his room and plucked at his lute forlornly. He had not finished one song when a voice interrupted him.

"I am sorry it had to be that way, skald."

Harald's wife stood behind him, wearing a white silk dress. Her bright green eyes were full of warmth and a smile was on her lips.

"My husband does what he can to provide peace," she said. "Although I defend him often, I am afraid that I am not particularly close to him."

Brand stopped playing. "What do you mean?"

"Does it surprise you that we have no children?" she said. "I tell the people I am barren, and that Brand's sister-in-law Kenna must bear the heirs, since Harald refuses to remarry. But the truth is—as a... *man*— Harald can only get stiff in the brothel. Something about commoners... something about the filthy whores that attracts him more than me... a noblewoman of the south who's been told often of her beauty."

"You're from the south?" Brand said. He wondered why in Varda she was telling him this.

"I am from the south," she said. "I have learned your tongue and have strived for years to speak it without an accent. I come from the capital city—the bad—of Zaros. It lies down the coast. The city is far larger than this port and sometimes I do miss it... the Yule celebrations, the grand palace, the warm summers and crisp autumns."

"A city larger than Andarr's Port?" Brand said. He didn't think that was possible.

"Far larger," she said. "I have told you all this, and you do not know my name. Or do you?"

"I do not, milady," Brand said.

"I am Alysse," she said. "It is not a Badelgard name, as I'm sure you can tell. You are a master of words." She sat down beside him. "And a master of other things, perhaps?"

The suggestion was vague, yet its meaning was cemented by the fire in her eyes. "My lady," Brand said, "if you mean to seduce me, I do not wish to betray Harald. You are his wife and I should not wish to get on his bad side. I know well from today what happens to those who get on his bad side."

"He would not mind," Alysse said. "You can even ask him." She smiled. "I will not pressure you to do such a thing, though, my good skald. I have never born him a child because of his perversion... his affinity for common whores. The women of The Cathouse call him the Brothel Sire. Lucky women they are, to lie with a man of noble status, when they are all so lowly."

"And have you been with other men?" Brand said.

"I would not ordinarily tell anyone this," Alysse said. "Only my husband knows; yet I can sense you have a good, trustworthy heart. The answer, I'm afraid, is yes. I have lain with a warrior of mine, Ragni. He died a few months ago of a wound and now I have no one to fulfill my passions."

"Did you have any children?"

"I have had two sons with Ragni," said Alysse. "They were blonde-haired like their father and unlike Harald, and I am a worrier. I hid from public view... sent them away to become priests at Dragonmount." She touched Brand's shoulder. "If you change your mind about me, dear Brand, let me know. There will be no repercussions; Harald will not care at all, and you may ask him."

Yet asking a man's permission to bed his wife was not an acceptable by any means and—in any man of normal character—would not be received well.

At lunch they had a snack of honey loaves, and a helping of fresh farmers' cheese. Brand played several songs for them—all happy, joyful songs of summer and love. The dark, frightening ones were fit for night, as Harald explained, against the wishes of young Stenn.

A little after noon, Brand asked if Harald would let him visit the city of Andarr's Port.

"Yes," Harald said. "Furthermore, you may have ten silvers as payment. Spend it however you wish… go see the dancers or the fire-eaters… watch a play in the theater. Go to the Cathouse or the Pleasure Palace; I hear the Lion's Den is in a terrible state."

Kenna glared at her brother-in-law from her seat.

"Only, do not listen to musicians," Harald said. "You must preserve your own style and not corrupt it with other instruments. I don't want you to come back with a shawm or a blaring horn. A voice and a lute is what I should want for my family."

Servants had shoveled the walk to the castle, but in town, snow reached the windows of the houses. A cold wind blew out of the sea from the northeast, making the air burn against Brand's partially exposed neck. He struggled through the snow and in time reached the crudely-shoveled marketplace. Noticeably fewer vendors stood out here hawking their wares; there were still some, but many had packed up shop. So, too, had the crowd dwindled; Brand assumed that most were inside huddling by the fire.

"I have never seen a storm like this in Andarr's Port," he heard a man saying. "Maybe in Ostergard or Trowheim. Maybe in Frostfall. But never here."

"I hear it's worse further east," a woman replied. "My boy was trying to visit his cousins on the farm—just a few miles off the main road—but there was too much snow."

Brand looked around. He was right in front of The Cathouse. The vulgar image that hung above the door—a naked woman and man in a lovers' embrace—aroused him. So, too, had his conversation with Alysse brought his lust to the fore of his mind. He wondered what The Cathouse offered that Harald couldn't find in Alysse. He could resist no longer.

A piece of paper was glued to the door. "One silver," it read, "for a good time." "Two silvers for a great time." "Ten silvers for the time of your life."

Brand gulped and looked around. No one was looking at him; no one would know about his surrender to temptation.

For ten silvers—the time of his life—Brand got a dark-haired beauty named Volina. During the periodic breaks in lovemaking, he asked her about her life. She seemed surprised that any of her clients would care.

"It gets tough sometimes," she said in a strange accent Brand didn't recognize, her shapely body dripping with sweat. "Last night it was cold—terrible cold. And my last client of the evening… he came in through my door. An' he was a young one, an' his skin was pale… paler than even you Badelgard people. An' he just stared at me with these eyes of yellow for minute and minutes… an' then he bit me… s'pose he is an aggressive one… and then he said, 'Tomorrow night we'll all be coming for you.'"

He got back to the keep later than he had hoped. The sun was setting in red over the sea. Out on a glass-walled porch—a priceless marvel not even King Sven possessed—Harald had a piece of canvas on an easel, and was hard at work painting the setting sun. Judging from half-finished painting—the sun and its reflection—he had done a competent job, even if he had no great artistic ability.

"Good work, milord," Brand said from behind.

"I have done many pictures," Harald said without looking back. "Pictures of the aspens in the family wood; pictures of my nieces and nephews; pictures of my brother Ivarr; pictures of my naked wife… I'm no real talent. I wish I were like the great Ranoul from the south. He was common, but he had talent. Me?" He paused. "I was just born into my greatness."

"The gods gave you your noble blood," Brand said, "just as they gave Ranoul his talent."

"And as they gave you yours," Harald said. "But with your talent, you can play songs. I just sit on a soft-cushioned throne and rule the city best as I know how, and as best as I know the wishes of the High King." He paused, dipping the brush in a red dye and then darkening the red sun. "The gods gave me the throne. The gods liked me enough to make me a Riverhall. And I suppose the gods despise the common."

"I hope not," Brand said. "I don't wish to live in such a world."

Harald kept painting.

"Did my friend come back?" Brand said. "I heard the roads were rough outside the city—impassible even. I thought perhaps you portsmen weren't used to such hard traveling."

"My men are perfectly capable of getting through snow," Harald said. "They are probably there now."

That night, the cooks doled out large bowls of mutton stew, and steins of dark winter ale. Brand sipped down the bitter drink with equal bitterness as he thought of Hilda.

"You have no honor, boy." Better than being dead. Yet Hilda's certain death made him feel guilt as much as letting her kill Gunnar.

Harald guzzled his stein, and then slammed it on the armrest. "You are in my court now, boy," he said. "You are a skald of the House Riverhall."

Brand mumbled assent. He needed to go after the Hilda's trail. He couldn't live with the knowledge he hadn't gone to die with her.

"What troubles you, skald?" Harald said.

"We have treated you perfectly well," Kenna said in a cold tone. "We have treated you as our equals, though I gather you are common."

Brand stood up. "I cannot live, knowing that I betrayed Hilda. I cannot live, knowing that I let you take her away, and I didn't follow after her."

"You'd be a fool to throw away all you've gained in my court," Harald said. "I have given you much. I have given you wine and good food, and hope for a good life. If you want to be placed back on the Hangman's List, or delivered to White Wolf Keep with your friend, I'm sure that can be arranged." There was no emotion in his voice.

Brand opened his mouth for a retort, then decided against it. Wisdom over honor. "I am ungrateful," he said. "I will serve you from here on, I swear."

"You swear?" Harald said, and then stood up, the gold of his coronet shining in the torchlight. "Will you take an oath of service to the House Riverhall? I must warn you; if you take the oath and break it, you will be executed as a traitor."

Brand hesitated. The words that came out of his lips were, "Yes."

"You will swear an oath to me, the Lord Baron?" Harald said. "And both to my family and to my noble house?"

"Yes," Brand said. His stomach twisted to knots at the thought of it.

"I will make you an honorary member of the nobility," said Harald. "I will appoint you housecarl, and you will from then on be known as Sir Brand."

"Will you grant titles of nobility as freely as you give your love to whores?" hissed Lady Kenna.

Harald snapped his head toward her with bared teeth, his eyes filled with rage. "You are not even my sister, Lady Kenna. You were my brother's wife, but if you test my mercy I fear you will be disappointed." He glanced back at Brand, then stood up and drew his sword. "This is the sword of my father, and his father before him. It is the sword of the House Riverhall—the Riverblade—and with it I will make you a housecarl, if you will say an oath."

Brand nodded and stood up and walked in front of the throne. Lady Alysse was smiling. Harald laid the flat of the Riverhall blade on Brand's shoulder. "Repeat after me," said Harald. "I, Brand…"

"I, Brand…"

"Pledge to be honorable and just."

"Pledge to be honorable and just."

"I swear fealty to the House Riverhall," Harald said, "and I pledge my utmost loyalty to them, and leave my life at their mercy."

Brand had trouble with that last line. "I swear fealty to the House Riverhall and I pledge my utmost loyalty to them, and leave my life at their mercy."

"I will fight for them, if my lord requires, and serve them until the day I die…"

Brand gulped and hesitated. Then he repeated it. "I will fight for them, if my lord requires, and serve them until the day I die…"

"I will do whatever the Lord of the House Riverhall wishes me to do, and never argue."

Brand had a feeling that line wasn't really in the oath. "I will do whatever the Lord of the House Riverhall wishes me to do, and never argue."

Harald smiled. "And I, Harald Riverhall, Baron of Andarr's Port and Guardian of the Sea, grant Brand the honor of a noble warrior, and from hereon he will be called Sir Brand, Riverhall Housecarl."

CHAPTER SIXTEEN

The night's feast was interrupted when Captain Erik of the River Guard ran in. He was pale-faced and panting hard. "My lord Riverhall," he said, "There are things climbing over the city walls. We have only a garrison of a hundred troops, your lordship, and these intruders are like none I've ever seen."

"Lock the castle doors!" Harald said.

"Why don't we send our little housecarl to defend us?" said Lady Kenna.

"Shut your mouth, Kenna," Harald said. "The boy is not trained in a sword, and the sound of a lute in the darkness will not protect from invading men."

"They are not men, milord," said the watch captain. "They are white as snow... they are grown men, grown women, little girls and little boys, mature and immature; and they all fight with equal ferocity. Half my men have been slain and we have only cut off the heads of a dozen; they are terribly strong, although they bear no armor or swords."

"Shut the doors!" Harald repeated at a shout. "And you stay here to protect us."

"I will not abandon my men!" the captain said.

"Yes, you will," Harald commanded.

"I won't!" The captain turned and ran for the door.

Harald drew out the Riverhall sword with a metallic ring. "Take one more step, Erik," he said, "and I will put you on the Hangman's List." The captain stopped. "I will peel your skin like an apple, and douse your wounds in salt."

Brand shivered at the words.

The captain turned around. "Yes, lord." He knelt with a hand on his pommel. "I will not disobey you, Your Honor."

"Good," Harald said. "Now... lock the doors."

The winds howled outside. The little girls wept in fright. Of the

Riverhalls, only young Stenn had brandished his sword and talked eagerly of charging into the evil night.

Brand walked up to Harald, realizing he could not withhold what he knew any longer. "Milord," he said, "I know what lies outside the castle walls."

"What are they?" asked Harald. Brand could sense fear even through his outward, manufactured sternness.

"They are darklings," Brand said. "A witch—one of the Ulfr— has reanimated the dead. They serve under her."

"There are two things wrong with your statement, boy," Harald said. "Firstly, the Ulfr have all died out. Secondly, the dead cannot fight." He frowned. "And thirdly, look! You're scaring the girls."

I'm scaring you, Harald.

"They were already scared," Brand said. "And the dead can fight. I have been to the land of Blackfold, in a den of an Ulfr witch."

"And did you see the dead fight?" Harald scoffed.

"No," Brand said. "I did not see them in Blackfold; there, I only felt them. But I saw them in the Darkling Wood."

"What do you suggest we do, boy?"

"They retreat at daylight," Brand said.

"Where do they go?" Harald said.

"In graves; in the clouds. Or to another world! Hell take me if I know," Brand said. "Tomorrow, in the morning... I think we should leave."

"Leave?" Lady Kenna shrieked. "Leave our riches and our fair port? Leave our castle? Our ancestral home? Our sacred wood?" She laughed bitterly. "You don't know what you speak of, boy."

Harald scratched his beard in thought. "He may be right, sister-in-law," he said. "But where would we go?"

"To Oskir... to somewhere that has an army!" Brand said.

"We can't make the journey to Oskir in a day!" Harald said, and laughed.

"If we all ride horses, and leave at first light, and ride hard and fast; perhaps we could get there in one day," Brand said.

"I doubt it, boy," Harald said. "And three of our horses are gone."

"What about Trowfell Keep to the south?" Brand suggested.

Harald was silent for a while. "The Trowfells do have an army, if a small one. But the House Trowfell is not well respected. Besides… I am not so eager to leave my court."

"Then let's wait until morning," Brand said, "and we'll decide then."

There was scratching on the door. "Let me in!" a voice screamed from outside. "Let me in. Please!"

Captain Erik moved to open it.

"Take another step and I will cut off your head." Harald's voice was stern.

The captain turned around, grimacing, obviously struggling with the command. "I obey you alone, Your Honor," he finally breathed as the sounds of screaming and tearing flesh echoed through the hall.

Harald's face was expressionless as the man was torn apart outside the castle door. Lady Kenna's eyes were narrow and a hint of a smile was on her lips.

The sounds of battle continued an hour afterward, and then the winds grew so strong that the only audible sound outside was howling. Brand retreated to his bed early that night; no one was in the mood for song, and neither was he in a fit state of mind to play for them. He wrapped himself in covers as the air—even inside the well-heated castle—dropped in temperature. Soon, wrapped in the thick furs of his bed, his breath crystallized into white fog.

Harald was at his door. "Sir Brand," he said, "You have a big day tomorrow. You are housecarl, and you will walk alongside me into the town that the strangers have savaged. The entire Guard is coming with us."

Brand nodded. "It will be my honor," he said. Yet something else struck Brand as odd. "It seems you aren't bothered by the peoples' deaths."

"I lied to you," Harald said, his breath also turning to white fog. "I said the earl's first job is to be liked. The earl's first priority is to himself. Many of the people may die, but if their leader dies—me—then it is all for naught; the swine cannot live without a swineherd."

"They can," Brand said, "but they turn into savage boars."

Harald nodded. "And the people also."

"Go through every longhouse," Captain Erik instructed the next morning, wearing his gold-colored armor and carrying a torch in his hand. "Peer into every dark room. Break into every airtight larder, every closet and crate and pot—everything the light does not touch. Thrust your torch within and if one of the darklings is in them, then savagely cut him to ribbons."

With those words of instruction, Brand, the whole Guard, and Stenn and Harald Riverhall, left through the castle gates—walking past the shredded corpse of the watchman at the gate—and entered a frigid, wintry, and thoroughly silent scene. The snow reached up to Brand's waist; the castle walk had not been shoveled. They waded through the snow together, feeling it moisten their breeches. It took them several minutes of struggle before they reached the first few longhouses of Andarr's Port. Or what remained of Andarr's Port.

Crimson splotched the snow in front of them. In the stain, buried halfway in the snow, was the mutilated body of a grown man, his arms and limbs gone from his body. Obviously he had tried to flee to the castle, but failed. A darkling had caught him; a savage, hungry beast that had torn off his limbs and took them away to gnaw.

"Do not take anything you see in the houses," said Lord Harald.

"It all is the property of the court. That includes Stenn, Sir Brand, and me. The Guard is the protecting force of the city, and of the throne; they shall not be greedy, or their hands shall be prevented from stealing again."

Brand had never been part of any court, nor had he ever had the title "sir." It would take some getting used to; he still felt much lesser in stature than even the members of the River Guard. But Harald had taken an interest in him, and made him an honorary member of the court. The reasons for it were beyond Brand's understanding, and it was a lightning-flash of luck; but sometimes he wondered what his father would say if he were still alive. He had been resentful toward the noble warrior houses; even hateful toward them. And what would he think of calling his son Sir Brand? He would probably refuse to address him in that way at all.

First of the buildings he checked was The Cathouse. Harald, curiously, came with him; but he was a notorious user of this filthy den. The door was locked—and with good reason—so Brand tried to kick down the door. He failed, and had to watch in embarrassment as Harald kicked it down for him.

Blood spattered the walls in The Cathouse. The body of a blonde whore lay there, her chest open and bloody. The savagery was difficult to take in.

"Kateryn, love," Harald said. "What a buttocks the world has lost."

Brand looked at Harald. "Surely there is something else about her that you can celebrate."

"Perhaps. But I've only seen her in body; never talked with her," Harald said.

Brand would not disrespect the dead; not common whores, either, who had hard lives serving the gutter of mankind. While Harald poked through a dark room, he made for Volina's chamber and saw that the door was shut and locked.

Brand knocked. "Hello? Volina?"

"Don't come near me, you sick, twisted monsters!" screamed the voice of Volina, obviously hysterical with fear and self-preservation. "I've killed three of you and I swear, I will cut your head off and stick it on a wooden stake if I must have to."

"It's Brand."

"Who?"

"You know. I paid for your services last afternoon."

"What do you talk about?" Volina said. She was wheezing and obviously in tears. "I have served many clients and cannot remember a single one."

"Maybe if you open the door, you'll remember."

"Why should I trust you?" Volina said. "What if you're one of them? I do not know if you are one of them!"

"I am human," Brand said. "Those darklings were not."

"*Dark-links*?" Volina said. "Is that what you call them?" She paused. "In my country, we call them the dead walkers… people brought back to life by a bad wizard-man, but not really back to life because they do not think, only eat."

"Open the door, Volina."

The peephole in the door opened, revealing Volina's chestnut eyes. A few seconds later, the door opened to reveal Volina. Her humble gray dress was torn up and shredded, as if in a struggle. Dried blood was caked over her body. "I remember you," she said, hands trembling. "You are a good man…" She fell onto him and began weeping. "You talked to me like I were a person, not just a whore."

Brand patted her back. "There, there," he said. "It's going to be all right."

"These are not like the dead walkers of my country," she said, occasionally choking on her tears. "In my country, the undead do not enter the huts… they only eat the fools who leave that safety, or if they make angry the bad wizard-men that created them. These… these *dark-*

links… they have no respect. They enter, an' they bash down the doors of the huts." She paused and wiped her tears with her ragged sleeve. "One thing, I think, they have in common; the dead walkers of my country and these *dark-links* hate fire, and they can't stand light. It blinds them, and it hurts them. They hide at day—always together, clustered together, 'cause there is strength in their numbers."

"Where do they hide?" Brand said.

"In dark places," Volina said, "as dark as they can find it."

Harald appeared, walking out of a door and up to them. "I have found nothing. The darklings aren't hiding here."

"Volina here says that they all hide together, in dark places—as dark a place as they can find," Brand said. He stepped away from her and grabbed her shaking hand. "Is there any pitch-black place in town?"

Harald shoved his sword back into the scabbard. "I do not ordinarily take advice from common whores," he said, "but if Violina—"

"Volina," she growled.

"—knows of the darklings, then I do know such of a place. The port has a church to a god—a very strange god, which no upland Badelgarder has heard of, but dear to the portsmen's hearts—and there are no windows. The worshipers sing and pray in total darkness."

"What god is it?" Brand asked.

"Umbra, Lord of Hidden Places," Harald said. "He is an import from the south, and an uncommon god even there. However, he has acquired quite a sizeable following here; though I—more a connoisseur of southern things than most Badelgard nobles—do not wholly approve of his worship."

"Do southern gods often find their way here?"

"Sometimes," Harald said, "but Umbra was brought by my dear wife. She is a devout worshipper of Umbra and built his church."

As they left, Volina knelt beside the body of the blonde whore that lay in the hall, and cried. "Oh, my sweet Gerta, I will miss you."

Harald gathered his nephew, as well as Captain Erik and the rest of his Guard; and together, with Volina, they made for the Church of Umbra. It was on the edge of the city, toward Riverhall Forest and overlooking the grey sea. It was not built in the common style of Badelgard houses: Rather than short and long, it was square and tall. Southern script—which Brand could not read—was written above the door. Indeed, there were no windows to let in the sun's light.

"The Guard shall enter first," said Harald.

"And me, too!" Stenn said.

"No," Harald said. "You are a Riverhall, and the only legitimate heir to the throne."

If there will be a throne when this is all finished, Brand thought to himself.

Two gold-armored guards entered the door, and within thirty seconds of their entering there was the sound of claws against metal. They rushed out.

One said, "There are hundreds of them in there, Your Honor, packed tight as dirt."

"We must burn it," Harald said.

A few members of the River Guard gasped; doubtlessly worshipers of Umbra.

"My wife will be sad to see it gone," Harald said. "And, if he is not already dead, so will the high priest. That strange man always frightened me, though." He pointed to the thatch roof. "Toss your torches upon it, Guardsmen. Let it burn, and let the darklings roast inside."

They obeyed and the savage beasts that lived within screamed, as shrill and high-pitched as whining tea kettles. They watched it burn until the screaming stopped, until all the darklings had burned to ash. Relief surged through Brand.

When they reached the open portcullis of the castle, Volina knelt before Harald and knit her fingers together. Tears streamed down her face and down her shapely neck, mixing with the caked blood of her lower body. "Let me come with you, milord. Let me come with you, I beg!" she said.

"The darklings are all dead," Harald said. "You will be safe."

"And what if they come back? There are rumors of other evils. A client from yesterday told me about them."

"Violina," Harald started, sounding slightly condescending.

"Volina!" she shrieked

"…you are not the kind of woman that stays in noble halls."

"Harald!" Brand snapped, overtaken with fury. "She has done so much for us. She may be a whore—even a common one—and she might not be the kind of guest you'd like in our halls. But by Vana, and by all the gods, and the Green Dragon, she's helped us. If there is any goodness in your heart, let her stay with us."

Harald stared at Brand for a few seconds.

"Don't let him talk to you like that, uncle!" Stenn said.

"No, Stenn," Harald said. "He is right. We shall listen to the housecarl. The girl stays, if it is what Sir Brand wishes."

Stenn grumbled.

"Thank you!" Volina shouted. "Thank you! You are the goodest earl in Badelgard!"

CHAPTER SEVENTEEN

Lady Alysse already knew about the burning of the church before they told her. "I have had a premonition of Umbra. The Lord of Hidden Places told me that his holy place has been defiled!" she said, standing up from her throne in her billowing green gown. "Then I walked out into the glass porch, and I saw smoke wafting into the air. What have you done, husband? What have you done?" Twin tears ran down her fair cheeks.

"I have done what is necessary, my lady," Harald said calmly, apparently unbothered by his wife's hysteria. "The darklings were hiding in the Church of Umbra; and therefore, the only solution was to set it aflame."

"For twelve years I've been wed to you," Alysse said, wiping the tears with her gold-dyed sleeve. "After my father, the bloody Duke of Voraigne, sent me off to this port. I build Umbra a holy church, and you defile it. You burn it! The last token of my origins, of the religion of my father and mother!"

"I am sorry," Harald said. "It was either let my fair lady die, or let the church of Umbra burn."

"I wish I had burned inside of it," Alysse said coldly. "Twelve years! Twelve years without love." She ran off, away from the throne room, and vanished out of sight.

The servants looked at Harald, unsure what to do.

"Cook the evening meal," answered the Lord Baron. "Make spiced lamb—her favorite—and bring her as many bottles of wine as she will drink. Do the best you can to make her feel at home."

Brand led Volina to a small guest room right outside the throne. "Will you have me now?" she asked, lying on the bed.

"No," Brand said, "but—"

"I am in no state to be had," Volina said.

"Rest, then," Brand said. "You'll need it."

She pulled the covers about her.

"Are you feeling all right?" Brand asked.

"No, but I'll manage. I always do."

"Will you turn into one of them?" Brand confessed the thing that had been on his mind.

"In my country, those bitten and scratched by the dead walkers do not turn into them," Volina said.

Brand breathed a sigh of relief; yet whether the girl was telling the truth, or saving her own hide, was uncertain.

That night, they had a meal fit for the world's most decadent glutton. They had spiced lamb—like Harald ordered—and also fried boar-rinds, baked potatoes smothered in cream, endless strips of bacon, and the richest honey-cakes Brand had ever tasted. With it they had bottles of wine—a drink Brand only had a few times before, because grapes did not grow in Badelgard—and the traditional mead.

Lady Alysse returned from her brooding and the dinner seemed to have only slightly lessened her animosity toward her husband.

"Where is Volina?" Harald said.

"She is sleeping," Brand said. "The wounds have made her tired."

Harald popped a boar-rind in his mouth and washed it down with wine. "Play us a song. You are housecarl, but you are a skald yet."

Brand retrieved his lute from his room. He stood before the half-drunk Riverhalls and played a song of frolic and light.

There is a house on a heavenly mountain
Bread like grass; mead in a fountain
Fight all day, feast all night
Altgard, home of honor and might

Brand bowed and they cheered wildly.

The night dragged on, but one by one, sleep took the Riverhalls. Lady Kenna and the girls went to bed first. Brand, Lady Alysse, Lord Harald, and Stenn remained awake. Eventually, long after dark, Brand bade them goodbye and went to his bedroom.

He was thinking of Hilda when Alysse appeared at his bedroom door. She was in her nightclothes, in a small dress that revealed a large portion of her breasts and almost all of her legs. Her forest-green eyes burned with desire. "My lord Brand," Alysse said. "You refused me once. But I won't let you refuse me again."

"My lady." Brand coughed. "I can't do this. I can't betray Harald."

She sat down by his bed. "My husband does not care. Why don't you understand that?" She stood back up and pulled her nightclothes over her head, revealing her fully unclothed form. She turned and shut the door, revealing her buttocks.

As lust flared up in Brand, he tried to look away. "My lady, please!"

"Do you find me ugly?"

"Not at all! You're a beautiful woman!"

"My husband doesn't love me," said Alysse. She began to cry. "I suppose no men do; not Harald and not you."

"I find you beautiful," Brand said, "but—"

"Then have me."

"I—" Brand started as Alysse walked over to him with a graceful yet seductive gait. He could not resist her any longer. The animal inside him was awakening. "Okay."

After they made love, Alysse very reluctantly left his side. Brand didn't want Harald to be suspicious, despite her protests that His Honor would not care.

Brand had not shut his eyes for a quarter hour when a loud commotion in the hall stirred him from his rest: someone, or something, was growling like a beast in the throne room. Had a wolf broken in somehow? That seemed unlikely.

"Back, demon!" shrieked the voice of Stenn. "Back! Now!"

Brand grabbed his sword and rushed out of his bedroom.

Stenn was in the throne room holding out his sword-blade defensively. Volina was circling around him like a hungry wolf, her sleek movements resembling those of some predatory animal. Sharp black claws had grown out of her fingers, replacing her fingernails. Her teeth were bared. Out of her throat came a low growling sound. Her eyes—black and soulless as a fly's—gleamed with hunger in the dim torchlight.

Brand had made a terrible mistake. Quickly, he joined Stenn's side, holding his sword with decidedly less skill than the young Riverhall. Volina let out a sharp, wolfish bark.

"The sickness has taken you," Brand said. "You once were a good woman, but now—"

"She once was a common whore!" Stenn said sharply. "And now she's a darkling, but she's still just a whore!"

Stenn let out a sharp cry and charged at her, slashing down with his sword. Volina sidestepped, quick as a mountain cat, and tackled him to the floor, scratching with her claws and biting with her teeth. She tackled Stenn to the ground.

Brand lifted his sword high above his head, ran forward, and brought the blade crashing down on Volina's neck. The darkling was so blinded by the ecstasy of feeding that she had lost her catlike reflexes. The blade cut through the neck and the head went flying, spurting blood onto Stenn's wounded body.

Stenn began shuddering and convulsing. He was badly wounded.

Barely a minute had passed before the entire Riverhall family was awake and running in.

"Great Umbra!" cried Lady Alysse.

"Dragon scales, we must find a healer!" Harald shouted.

Kenna rushed in and screamed, "It's the skald's fault! He told us to let the whore in! Let him be hanged!"

"I'm sorry," Brand said, and tears formed in his eyes. "I'm so very sorry. I didn't realize—"

"We will not hang a housecarl," Harald said. "We will find little Stenn a healer."

"These wounds are beyond the skill of any in our keep," Lady Kenna grumbled bitterly.

"Only at the High Temple of Vana could we find a healer who could purge such devilry, but that's too far away," Harald said. "That would take days of hard riding, and we only have one day before he turns into—"

"Don't say it!" shrieked Lady Kenna. "My boy will never turn into one of them."

"What of Trowfell Keep?" asked Alysse. "It is possible to make the journey in less than a day, if we ride hard."

"The Trowfells are poor and live in the mossland," Kenna said. "I will not have our family be associated with them."

"Then will you have your son die, Kenna?" Alysse sneered. "The Trowfells may not be as rich as we Riverhalls. But you know as well as I do of their Healing House, with its hot springs and expert physicians."

"Don't talk down to me, you southern slut," Kenna growled. "I see the way you eye men who aren't your husband."

Alysse laughed. "Southern, I may be. But my father is the Duke of Voraigne, and my mother the duchess; and with one one-hundredth of the gold in our coffers, we could buy all your family's holdings, Kenna

Wildsaber."

Kenna jerked toward her, as if to start a fight.

"Enough, ladies," Harald said, stepping in to block Kenna. "I won't have you quarrel. We make for Trowfell Keep now."

"No, we won't do that," Lady Kenna growled. "My son is too good for the Trowfells. We will ride to Wildsaber Keep and to my brother the earl. We go there, or we go nowhere."

There was scratching on the door.

"What is that?" Harald said.

"Milord," Brand said, "if I had to guess, I'd say that those who were stricken down yesterday have arisen as darklings."

"We leave at first light then," Harald said, then gave a sidelong glance to Kenna, "for Wildsaber Keep."

Kenna smiled.

CHAPTER EIGHTEEN

At first light, they retrieved all their horses from the lord's stables, and then fetched a few from the commoners' stables. Then, they left out of the city gate and bade goodbye to their ancestral home. Brand knew he would miss the easy living of Andarr's Port despite Hilda and Gunnar's accusation of its "southernness" and "luxury." Vana grant rest to their souls.

They continued for a few miles down the road on the north side of the river, following it due east, and reached the rocky river valley a short time later. Aspens grew everywhere except the road, but now the winds and frost had shaken off their leaves. Now they were naked and gray against the deep snow.

They passed several tiny fishing villages on the way—Utja Thorpe, Ormer Thorpe, Garn's Hole, and other unimportant settlements that Brand had never heard of. In the mad dash with Hilda, they had paid no attention to the villages they traveled past. Here there were plentiful farms: numerous apiaries, where bees were kept for honey and mead; fruit farms such as apple orchards and pear orchards; and, to a lesser extent, cereal farms where wheat and barley grew. All were snowy and silent in the winter, their color discarded.

Besides Brand and the Riverhalls, about twenty servants—and the twelve-strong Guard—traveled with them, creating a long caravan stretching across the road that surprised travelers. Brand felt safer than he would alone; vicious brown bears were known to live here, and they had acquired a taste for human flesh. Some people north of the main road—wild-men, as they were called—had a special reverence for them and cloaked their priest in brown bear hides. Among the wild-men, eating raw bear meat was considered to increase a man's vigor in battle and in bed.

The road turned into a bridge over water as they reached a swamp. The dark, frozen waters bled inland from the river. Giant sycamores—their leaves shed for winter—dominated the landscape.

Now, the swamps were frozen, but Brand knew that in the summertime, it would teem with life: frogs, water shrews, geese, ducks, and more. He had heard of the Waterwood, but never thought he'd get to see it for himself.

"The fishing is great in the Waterwood, or so I have heard. Trout and herring abound," Harald said. "It is all the domain of the Wildsaber family."

Brand, not sure of the exact distance between Andarr's Port and Wildsaber Keep, was surprised that they reached their destination before midday. The keep was built on a large circular hill—obviously artificial—that jutted out of the frozen water. The walls were built of wooden palisades, similar to White Wolf Keep. Numerous flags flew from the posts, bearing the coat-of-arms of the Wildsabers: a white swan against a yellow field, with two crossed swords in the upper right-hand corner.

They had not yet reached the gate when a pair of warriors rode up to them. Their tabards also bore the Wildsaber coat-of-arms. "State your business," one said.

"We are the Riverhalls," Harald said. "We do not need to state anything."

"I am Lady Kenna, and a Riverhall, but I am also a Wildsaber. My son is wounded. We must get him help. My brother is earl of this keep, so let us through at once."

"The keep has had trouble of late and the city has been closed to visitors for the past week," the guard answered. "But if you are a full-blooded Wildsaber, lady, I suppose you—and you alone—may have audience with the earl; you must remove all weapons, however. Our lord is distrustful of strangers of late; and for good reason."

Kenna removed a thick steel dagger at her side—her only weapon—and handed it to the guards. She rode off while the rest of the Riverhalls waited.

She returned an hour later, after her family had suffered a long while in the cold.

"My brother wants my son and my daughters, and them alone," Kenna said. "Only my children and I may stay in the keep." She glared fierily at Alysse. "I suppose he does not want any southern sluts in his hall."

"And what of us?" said Harald. "Surely you don't mean to leave us out here in the cold."

"He believes you have failed me as a brother-in-law," Kenna said. "However, if you disband the River Guard, swear fealty to him—"

Harald laughed darkly.

"—strip yourself of your titles, become a lowly housecarl of the Wildsabers, then he will accept you into the keep and grant you whatever minimal provisions you require to survive."

Harald drew his sword out of the sheath with a wild ring. "You insult me, she-wolf! Guards…"

"Kill her!" Alysse screamed.

Brand was inclined to agree with her command.

"No," Harald said. "Don't kill her. Kill her son. And give her daughters scars, that they may become even uglier than they already are."

A large group of Wildsaber guards started riding out of the gate. They were, perhaps, forty strong, dressed in chainmail and bearing heavy spears.

"The River Guard is strong, she-wolf," Harald shouted. "Twelve of my Guard are stronger than all of your impoverished, backwater Wildsaber soldiers combined."

"I wouldn't test it," Kenna sneered. "Give me my children now, 'Lord' Harald."

"You win for now," Harald said. "I may prefer the luxury of the port. But I will take vengeance upon you, she-wolf. You married my brother, but you never were and never will be a Riverhall."

"That is a good thing," Kenna said.

"I am not a true Riverhall," Brand said, speaking from his heart and his heart alone. "I have been across Badelgard, however. I have seen many cities in my time. I have been to White Wolf Keep… and this… this pitiful wooden keep of the Wildsabers is the worst I've ever seen. You call Lady Alysse a slut… she is of a wealthy house. And you, Kenna, come from the dirtiest, most disgusting keep I have ever had the misfortune of seeing." Brand drew his sword and rattled it in the winter sun, and cried out, "Long live the Riverhalls!"

"Long live the Riverhalls!" the River Guard called after him.

"Long live the Riverhalls!" Harald cried, "and long live Sir Brand!"

Kenna's children rode out away from the Riverhall host, and Harald did not command the River Guard to kill them.

"May you always live in shame," Harald said. "Kenna, traitor to our house."

"I am a member of your house no longer," Kenna sneered, and rode off with the Wildsaber soldiers.

"I hope your son becomes a darkling and eats you tonight!" Harald said.

And Brand knew, in all likelihood, his curse would become reality.

They set up camp in the Waterwood, about ten miles south of Wildsaber Keep. The servants made a fire and set up tents. There Harald and Alysse sat around in the light of the crackling flame, and Brand joined them.

"I may prefer peace to war," Harald said, "but I will not bring such dishonor as to not retaliate. I have never liked my sister-in-law, but now I hate her."

"We will go to my father and bring back a hundred knights of Zarubain," Alysse said. "None can stand against their steel swords and thundering hooves."

"Let's go there!" Brand said. "Nothing will please me more to have revenge, though I am not a Riverhall."

"From now on, you are a Riverhall," Harald said. "I proclaim you more a Riverhall than Lady Kenna will ever be, and more a Riverhall than any of her children will ever be. If you have children, boy, then they will be Riverhalls!"

"Thank you, my lord," Brand said. "Thank you so very much." His face grew stern as he looked into the orange flame. "We should do as Alysse says... bring back an army and take vengeance on Wildsaber Keep."

"Come spring, we will," Harald said. "The ocean cannot be sailed in the winter—at least, not with the ships we currently have. And the Sky Cliffs cannot be climbed down; only the King's Drawbridge can take us to the southlands, and that has not been lowered in a long time. The High King will never lower it for us."

"So where shall we go?" Brand asked.

"Come with me, where we cannot be heard," Alysse said.

They walked under the shade of a large sycamore, away from the servants. There, Alysse whispered to Brand and Harald.

"My sons that I had with the warrior Ragni... they are probably big enough to hold a sword by now. We shall go to the Dragonmount and reclaim them. They shall be delighted to hear they are noblemen; and we shall find them wives. Thus, the line will be perpetuated."

"I did not realize Brand knew of our secret," Harald said.

Strange, Brand thought, that he did not care about Alysse's illegitimate children.

"Sir Brand is trustworthy," Alysse said. "Now... let us make for Dragon Temple."

"What will we tell the servants?" Harald said.

"We needn't tell them," Alysse said. "Half will go to Oskir and petition the High King for defense and aid. Half the Guard shall come with us; and Brand, our housecarl who has proven himself so very loyal."

"And if the Dragonpriest does not relinquish our sons' care?"

Harald said.

"He will," said Lady Alysse. "No one can refuse a duke's daughter."

"We will do as you say," Lord Harald said.

CHAPTER NINETEEN

At first light, Erik and five other members of the Guard, as well ten servants, left for Oskir and the High King's throne.

Lord Harald, Lady Alysse, Brand, six of the Guard, and ten other servants left for Dragonmount. They rode long and hard, following the river valley east. Around noon, they began an ascent up steep switchbacks and, after a ride that exhausted both horses and riders, reached the rocky upland area of Badelgard densely covered in spruces, firs, and pines. Snow buried the land up to the horses' knees.

They were now in Trowheim, the domain of the Blackhelms. Blackhelm Keep, overlooking Frost Lake, was just a short ride west. It was the domain of Gunnar's father. Brand reflected briefly on his friend and prayed he would honor his memory.

By the time darkness fell, they had reached the foot of the Dragonmount: An impossibly tall peak that distinguished itself from the others by its jaggedness and steel color.

It was here that the Green Dragon once rested; it was here that the father of Badelgard battled with him a day and a night. And it was here that, after becoming friends, they launched an all-out attack on the evil Ulfr, worshipers of a vile demoness. Riding on the Green Dragon, Buntringer had burned their cities with all-consuming dragonfire and driven them to extinction.

Or so it was said. Now, things were stirring in Badelgard that made Brand question the accepted legend. An Ulfr witch still remained; an army of dead walked behind her. There was a rumor that monsters walked the Ice Shelf.

The servants dispersed to gather kindling and firewood. They had brought provisions: smoked salmon and dry biscuits, and other travel fare. The rustic dinner took the edge off the hunger. Once the fire started, the servants put together the tents. Lady Alysse instructed the servants to set up the tents, and they obeyed in short order.

The Guard slept in one tent; the servants in another; and in the third tent, Alysse, Harald, and Brand. What happened next, Brand would never forget.

"Will you have me tonight?" asked Alysse, and shot him a fiery glare.

Brand gave a shocked look to Harald. "I'm sorry, Alysse. Harald—"

"Sir Brand, my housecarl," Harald said, "I do not care if you bed my wife. I do not care if you bed commoners, or priestesses of Vana, or painted whores. It makes no difference to me."

"You are a strange man, Harald," Brand said.

"I would not normally let a commoner say that, but you speak truth," Harald said. "And you are no longer common. So get on with the deed, Brand. Bed my wife—she's all yours."

"I take that back; you are a very strange man, Harald," Brand said. He looked down at the leather floor of the tent.

The next morning, they made a stern procession to Dragonmount. Throughout the whole ride to the rocky peak, Brand's mind swam with memories of last night.

What kind of lot have I fallen in with? A man who will not bed his wife but will let another have her. A man who executes criminals for the people's pleasure, yet does not shed a tear when the whole city dies.

Brand grunted. His legs were terribly sore from riding, and his back ached horribly. He wondered if being a commoner was better than living as a noble in this sort of company.

And yet, in many ways, they have been good to me.

They reached the base of the peak and there, against the rock, sat the Temple of the Green Dragon. It was a large building of dark stone, supported by thick gray pillars and capped with a domed roof.

"There is no beauty to this building," said Lady Alysse. "In my homeland, we decorate the pillars and make them pleasing to the eye with flutes and carvings. And we do not use such grim stone."

"You will have to make do with what we grim Badelgarders have," said Harald. "My people and your people are different; and yet, we are joined as one."

"In some ways we are, Harald. In others, not as much," Alysse said, then glanced at Brand knowingly and smiled at him.

Brand smiled faintly, then looked away in shame.

At the entrance of the temple, a shirtless, hairy-chested man met them. He was huge and had a thick brown beard and wild, uncut hair. In his large, meaty fist he clutched a torch. He wore crude leather leggings and hanging around his neck was an amulet in the shape of a dragon.

"What do you flatlanders want from the High Dragonpriest and his priesthood?" the man growled. "You're dressed as dandies in your fancy-woven kirtles and cloaks, and you look like you're off to some genteel party."

"Calm down, priest," Lady Alysse said. "You speak to a woman of noble blood."

"The junior priests are racing up the peak with stones on their backs," the High Dragonpriest said. "The trolls have returned to the Ice Shelf, and I am getting my boys ready for war, so I apologize for my barbed tongue, Your Honor. The evil of the Ulfr has returned... and the center of this evil comes from Oskir, and the High King's throne."

"Do not speak of the High King so," Alysse said.

"It is not the High King I speak of," the priest said. "It is something he possesses."

The Idol of the Great Mother. Brand shivered.

"What is your name?" Alysse demanded.

"I have no name but High Dragonpriest," the man said. "And yet, I have not yet asked you what you want of me. Why do you come to our temple of dragon's sons, fair lady of high birth? Why do you come with dozens of men in your retinue? This place is not fit for any but those with the toughness and spirit of dragons."

"My name is Alysse. Does that sound familiar?" she asked.

"I admit that it does," the High Priest said, "and yet, I do not know who you are."

"I come from Andarr's Port," Alysse answered. "Many years ago, I brought two blonde-haired, blue-eyed children to your temple. I travel here to reclaim my sons, Forni and Jarni."

The High Dragonpriest paled. He was slack-jawed for a moment, then said, "Forni is now known as Razorclaw; and Jarni as Whitefang. They do not know their original names, nor do they know of their high birth or anything about life outside the temple. They are some of my best junior priests, and better with a club than most any of their colleagues."

"They get it from their father," Alysse said.

"Perhaps," the High Dragonpriest said, "but I won't let you have them. I need them to fight the trolls on the Ice Shelf."

"You will let me have them," Alysse said. "They are blood of my blood, flesh of my flesh. They came from my womb. You have no claim to them!"

"You gave them to the Order of the Green Dragon, milady," High Dragonpriest replied, "and they will remain with the Order of the Green Dragon until their lord releases them."

"Then release them," Alysse snapped.

"I will not," the High Dragonpriest said. "Skruga, the Green Dragon, does not approve of their release."

"And how do you know that?" Alysse said. "How do I know you're just imagining what he's saying?"

"Milady," Harald started.

"Don't 'milady' me, Harald," Alysse said. She looked back. "Guards, arrest him."

The River Guard hopped off their horses, gold armor glinting in the sun, and drew their sharp steel swords. They waded through the snow over to the Dragonpriest.

The Dragonpriest let out a wild cry and blew into the torch. Fire spurted out like dragon-flame, and struck a guard, singeing his moustache. The Dragonpriest dropped the torch and drew a steel club from behind his back. "Skruga, grant strength! Ooh aye! Ooh aye!"

The guards circled around him, blocking any outward movement. They moved in and struck with their swords; he swung hard and bashed a guard in the helmet. No sooner had he done that than another member of the Guard moved in and disarmed him.

"The Order of the Green Dragon can fight trolls and the ghosts of the Ulfr," said Lady Alysse, "but they cannot fight well against the River Guard."

"You have disarmed me and put me to shame," the Dragonpriest said. He seemed genuinely crushed. "This I will grant you: you may stay at the temple awhile, and if Razorclaw and Whitefang wish to come with you, then I won't stop them. Nothing more I can promise. If they do not wish to come, that is their choice."

"I know they will come with me," Alysse said. "What kind of fools would want to live in a place like this when they could live in a castle overlooking the sea?"

The junior priests returned in late afternoon. There were about twenty of them: big, lumbering brutes with muscular chests and powerful arms gained by years of hard work. It was obvious to Brand which ones belonged to Alysse: two boys—perhaps nine years old—running side by side, with the blonde hair, light eyes, and button noses of their mother; and the large chins, stern features, and huge shoulders of another— Ragni.

"Milady," the Dragonpriest said, "this is Razorclaw, and this is Whitefang."

The twin boys looked at her in confusion. Alysse embraced them one after the other.

"My sons!" she said, half-crying. "My beautiful sons."

"Mother?" they said in unison.

"Yes," she answered them. "I am your mother. I am Alysse and—" She looked back; the servants were staring at them and she jabbed a thumb at Harald. "—your father is this man."

"Alysse?" said Razorclaw, who was a bit larger than his brother. "You are dressed like a rich woman."

"She is a rich woman," Harald said from behind, "and I am a rich man. We are of the House Riverhall."

"So you have a lot of gold?" Whitefang asked.

"Yes, that is what 'rich' means," Harald said. "And it is all yours. You must come with us, and we will shower you with gold."

"Gold is useless," Whitefang said. "Gold makes bad weapons— it can't kill trolls, and it can't stop the Ulfr from coming back."

Brand had a feeling these two were so sheltered from the outside world they would not go easily.

"Gold is not useless," Alysse said, her tone becoming sharper. "Gold can buy things. Gold can buy food, and houses, and fighting men. If you buy fighting men, you can fight trolls and stop the Ulfr from coming back. Gold can buy anything."

"It can't buy anything here," said Razorclaw.

The other junior priests left into the temple; apparently they had grown bored of the conversation. Of them, only the Dragonpriest and the twins remained.

"In the lowlands, it can buy anything," Alysse said, smiling outwardly but her tone growing sharper with irritation. "It can buy a pig, or a goat... it can buy butter-roasted crab... it can even buy a sword!"

"Swords can't split open troll-scales. You have to bash them," Whitefang replied. "We have clubs."

Alysse sighed. "Oh. You two definitely need to be taught some lessons about the outside world."

The Dragonpriest interrupted. "Go on, you two."

Razorclaw and Whitefang left into the temple.

"The temple is relatively small," the Dragonpriest said. "The heating isn't the best. But inside, we have some scrapings of food, and guest quarters for a few; but not enough for all of you."

Harald turned around and shouted, "The River Guard and all the servants will sleep in the tents. Set them up."

Immediately inside the stone walls of the temple was a blazing pyre. It burned in a great central fire pit.

"This is the Ever-Burning Flame," said the High Dragonpriest. "It represents the powerful fire which the Green Dragon rained down upon the Ulfr. I require my junior priests to keep it burning at all times—it's a symbol of our people's hope."

"And there seems to be very little hope in this bleak place," Alysse said. "Perhaps the warmth and brightness of such a flame is all you really have in this frozen wasteland."

"There is joy in working in the fields, and there is joy in fighting and spilled blood, my lady," said the High Dragonpriest. "There is joy in dragging bags of stones up the mountains…"

"I do not think that would make me happy," Harald said.

"That's because you're a fair-skinned nobleman who never gets out in the sun," the High Dragonpriest began, "and your hands have no blisters, and you ride around on costly horses and wearing costly clothing. Until you know what it is like to serve the Green Dragon, though, boy, you have never felt true joy—only luxury."

Brand had a hard time believing such difficult work and strenuous living conditions could bring joy, and he pitied anyone who could.

"You'd best be careful with your insults," said Harald. "Remember what the River Guard did to you, despite your spitting dragon-fire."

"And you, highborn, remember the mission of our priesthood—to protect Badelgard from the Ulfr, and guard the sacred Dragonmount. Let us both have respect," he replied.

Passing the priests' quarters, the rooms were of shabby stone and boasted only straw beds and chamber pots. Brand felt uneasy until he got to the guest rooms—of which there were four. They had modest furnishings compared to even a middling commoner's house, yet extravagant furnishings compared to the priests' quarters. They had wooden beds with feather mattresses, chamber pots, desks, and small, unadorned closets.

The relief was only slight. There was something so bizarre about the way Harald let Brand have his wife, and though Hilda was a thief, a killer of men, and a general vagabond—Vana grant her rest—Brand had been happier in her company. A thorny rose she had been, but a rose. And Gunnar... he did not even want to think about Gunnar, his best friend and bonded warrior.

For dinner, they had brown bear stew—a meal of heavenly richness compared to the meager travel fare they had eaten of late. The Dragonpriest then hauled in a large keg of mead. "This is rough stuff," he grumbled, "and not what you lowlanders are used to. But it gets the job done, and there's plenty of it. When the Green Dragon Priests prepare for war, we drink mead like oxen drink water."

And it was true; the Green Dragons were a warrior order more than a priestly order. Unlike the pacifist, all-female Priesthood of Vana on the southwestern edge of the Sky Cliffs, the Priests of the Green Dragon made war on many: on earls who did not pay tribute; on earls who made an insulting comment; on earls who looked at the High Dragonpriest the wrong way on one of his occasional visits. Now, they would fulfill their traditional war duty: to extinguish the Ulfr threat rising on the Ice Shelf and in the whole of the nation.

CHAPTER TWENTY

Escape was not an easy proposition; he needed a horse. All of the horses were protected by the River Guard outside the temple, both by day and by night, and the gods knew he could not defeat one of them, nor lullaby them to sleep. And he was not entirely sure he wanted to escape from Alysse and Harald: should he really retreat? He was a housecarl, now, and had escaped his lowly position as a common swineherd's son. And Lady Riverhall was certainly—if not beautiful—comely in face and shapely in form. It was only Harald that was a strange bird.

Thus, three long weeks passed and Brand remained in the Dragon Temple as Alysse ceaselessly tried to convince her bastard sons to leave with her. Winter's cold deepened and even the fire could not warm Brand's bones. Though they were certainly not in any state of luxury, Yule Eve arrived, and the High Dragonpriest decorated the grim stone abode with holly and mistletoe. Even here, in this icy, snowy hell—on the darkest day of the year—they attempted to appease the Yule ghosts.

Brand stood in his room, deeply cold and having just debated the merits of escaping for the past hour. Alysse appeared behind him; he could smell the perfume, which she wore even in this frozen wasteland.

"Brand," she said. "I have good news."

Brand turned around. "What is it, milady?" he said.

"I have not bled at all this month," Alysse said. "And I threw up in the morning. Do you know what this means?"

"No, milady," Brand said.

"I am with child," Alysse said. "And the child belongs to you. Your blood will further the next line of Riverhalls. Now we can depart these brutal, rabid bears of children... We can make for the warm lowlands. The Line of Riverhall will continue on, and it will be your blood that is in them."

A breathlessness overtook Brand, and sudden joy filled him. He smiled brightly. "That is wonderful news to hear, milady." Then he frowned. "Yet will there be a domain to give him? Will there be even a Badelgard for them to live in? What if the Ulfr witch succeeds?"

"The Green Dragons leave for the Shelf tomorrow," she said, "or so the High Dragonpriest has told me. Let's leave at the same time. We'll make for the lowlands. This weather is making me ill. I am so cold... so horribly cold. And I want the child in me to be well."

"And where will we stay?" Brand said. "We've been here three weeks, completely isolated... who knows if the darklings have spread? Who knows what has happened to the port? No news comes here. No people come here."

"We make for Oskir and will join Captain Erik," said Alysse. "Every noble family has a guest longhouse there. It isn't a long journey, either."

"It will be a long journey in the snow," Brand said. "It's a long journey in this weather—and without a fire to warm us, or a daily meal, at that."

That night, Brand sang a quiet Yule song as he strummed his lute. Due to the chill of the air, and the fatigue of the living conditions, his voice had grown hoarse. He sang anyway, as best he could:

The week of Yule comes once a year
Mistletoe is in the hall
Hunger none may fear
Gifts for the poor and lights for all

Alysse and Harald clapped weakly. The Green Dragons did not clap or cheer at all; they knew nothing of applause or thankfulness, and Brand furthermore doubted their ability to appreciate music.

The next morning, the warrior-priests left for the Shelf—running in a pack like wolves—long before the sun arose. The two children of Alysse left with them and she did not say goodbye.

The servants packed up their tents, and, together on horses, they began a long ride through deep snow and ice. The snow now reached the horse's bridles, and chilled their legs despite the long cloaks and thick kirtles and woolen breeches. With the warmth of Oskir at the fore of their minds, they continued on against the numbing cold—yet Brand did not know what to expect when he reached Oskir's famed Golden Gate.

It began snowing hard again late that afternoon. They continued through it, though the wind was unbearable. Soon afterward, they reached some kind of path—visible because of the tall wooden posts sticking out of the snow.

"We've reached the King's Road," said Harald. "We're not far off from Oskir."

They hurried down the road in hopes that they might reach the capital city before nightfall. The snow had grown almost unnavigable. Brand's horse began shivering underneath his legs.

The horses of Badelgard had thick coats and strong resolve. Yet even they could grow too cold and die. This snow—deep even for the uplands—slowed them down immensely, preventing them from gaining shelter.

Night fell quickly, as it did in winter, and the cold deepened. Even in his tunic, thick kirtle, and cloak, the chill seeped into Brand. His breathing became slow, erratic white puffs of fog. His joints stiffened despite his constant shivering. The cold filled him, deep and tender like a lover's embrace, and numbed his bones. He thought he might be dying; and yet, somehow, in this winter of death, he did not care.

Well after dark, a welcome sight appeared in the distance: lights on King's Hill. Now, the waters of the Great Falls were soundless: frozen in mid-run as they plunged into an equally frozen river far below. They had reached Oskir, the City of the High King. At the top of the hill sat the proud Golden House where His Highness lived, and just a few feet below sat Earls' Court and the longhouses of the noble families. Even the Baron of Andarr's Port—technically not an earl—had a residence there. Not in a thousand years did Brand think he'd ever be staying in Earls' Court, even for a short time.

The Golden Gate, oddly enough, lay open.

At the side of the street, a madwoman in rags called out to them. "All hail the High King! The King of Skulls! The King of Death! Cross him and die!" She bared her few rotten teeth and growled at them as they walked by. "In his hand is a statuette of gold. In his command is an army that does not eat, sleep, or die! And on his head is a crown!"

Brand was so numb from the cold that he did not react to her. But he did notice that the coat-of-arms of the Oster family—a golden rooster against a red field—had been replaced with a white skull against a purple field. That was an Ulfr symbol.

In the cold, all he could think about was reaching Earls' Court and sleeping by the fire. Yet he did not know, even if cast into a furnace, it would cure the chill inside him.

Brand awoke in the light of a blazing fire. It was silent, and the light of the sun filtered through glass windows

"The cold got to you," Harald said. "You nearly died."

"Dying in the cold," Brand said, "is worse than being peeled, or drawn-and-quartered, I imagine; but I don't want to do those either."

"The High King can do no such thing to you," Harald said. "You are a housecarl now. The worst thing that could happen to you is a beheading, and I won't let that happen. I swear on my honor."

Brand was still shivering. He rubbed his hands in the fire. Slowly, he stood up. They had wrapped a bearskin blanket around him but it didn't help much. "I don't think I'll ever be warm again," he said.

"Oh, you will," Harald said. "Give it a few more hours."

A plate sat on a nearby wooden table, offering the morning breakfast—three strips of crisp bacon and two boiled eggs—and a large stein of mead sat next to it. Outside the window, the snowflakes had stopped falling and the sun shone in the blue sky. The snow reached the window of the longhouse.

"And what of the High King, and the Golden House?" Brand asked.

"We have not yet seen him," Harald said, "nor have we been in the Golden House. He is not accepting visitors until dusk." Harald smiled. "It is no matter. We are safe and indoors, and the blizzard did not claim us."

"Where is Alysse?" Brand asked.

"My wife is resting in the other room. Had a bad morning sickness today," Harald said. "But it is good that we are safe in Oskir, and we needn't worry while the baby grows inside her."

Brand wasn't so sure. Worry seemed healthy in this situation.

"My wife has not taken a lover since Ragni died," Harald said. "Now she is content to be with child… now, hopefully, with dark hair like me. Your hair is dark like mine, after all." He smiled again. "If it is a son, he will be the next head of the House Riverhall. If it is a daughter, we will marry her to someone of Riverhall blood; the chief scoutmaster's son is only nine, and a nine-year discrepancy is not terribly much."

"Is he still alive?"

Harald frowned. "I don't know. Woodhome is filled with Riverhall-blooded scouts, and they are expert archers and swordsmen—skilled enough to rival the elves of the north."

"And what of Captain Erik and the rest of the River Guard?" Brand asked.

"He and his five men are outside," Harald said. "The High King would not grant audience with any lowborn, so he stayed in the Riverhall guesthouse until we made our return."

There was silence for a while. Brand awkwardly got up onto his feet and grabbed his plate of breakfast. As he turned to sit back down in front of the fire, he caught Harald's eyes staring at him.

"You have had my wife," Harald said. "She loves you, you know."

"Harald," Brand said, "you are a strange man."

"I am a strange man," Harald said. "I admit that full well. But you are strange as well. All sensitive artists are. I have never met a musician of normal disposition. Something about the humors, the blood and the bile…"

Brand grew uncomfortable. He placed an entire boiled egg in his mouth and chewed it, then washed it down with the mead stein.

"My wife speaks of you fondly," Harald said. "She speaks of you with more adoration than she did with Ragni."

"We don't need to talk about that, though, do we?" Brand said, and nibbled at some bacon. "You do understand… it is awkward for a man to discuss his affairs with the husband of the beloved. It simply isn't in accordance with the rules of courtly love."

"There is something between you and her that really makes for compatible humors," Harald said. "There is something there."

Brand took a big gulp of mead. "I do love her," he said, "but I do think that I am performing your duty for you. You are her husband; and yet you do not deliver what she wants… what the animal in her needs."

"I do have an affinity for the common and the whores among us," Harald said. "My wife knows this and does not care; nor does she get jealous of those grubby women who serve me. The whores among us are always so delighted to have a highborn as a client. Especially one such as me, who—dare I boast?—is handsome." He paused. "I do sense some tension, some unspoken fury in you and I believe that the feeling is against me. So therefore I must ask: What is this tension, Brand, between you and me?"

"Harald," Brand said, "I do not know what it is in Varda that you mean."

Brand set the remains of breakfast before the fire, stood up, and walked out the door into Oskir.

At twilight, Harald and Alysse—and Brand, having gathered his bravery—made their way across the snow to the Golden House. It was a huge longhouse—not especially tall, but wide and sprawling with several wings. The outer walls were painted golden and trimmed with white; the painting was redone every year to keep up its beauty.

The King's Guard was not at the door. In fact, the door was slightly open and creaking in the wind. A foul odor of rot billowed out of it. Lady Alysse covered her nose with her sleeve. "I will stay outside," she said. "I'd rather suffer in the cold…"

Harald nodded and kissed her hand. "Yes, lady love."

Together, Harald and Brand stepped through the door.

CHAPTER TWENTY-ONE

The windows of the Golden House had purple curtains, and the floors were layered in precious beeswax. Gold-lined candelabras once spread light through the king's residence, but now remained unlit, the wicks of their candles crumpled and black. The same nervousness Brand had felt in the witch's house returned, deep in his gut. He pressed on through it and led Harald into the huge throne room.

The walls were painted a lush green. The windows here were of fine glass, and the ceiling was higher than in any other longhouse in Oskir. A harp sat here, and a lute on a stand. Bearskins and deer skins lined the way to the High Throne. And there, on that large throne of yew, sat High King Sven; but it wasn't entirely Sven. In fact, only the jewel-studded High King's Crown on its head proved it was Sven.

It was a corpse: not a corpse you could distinguish features from, but instead a long-dead corpse. Sven's body bore such extensive rot that only Ulfr devil-craft could have advanced it that far. It was not wet, but instead dry and crumbling. In its sockets there were no eyes, yet Brand felt that it was staring at him.

"You have requested audience with the king, and he shall hear your requests," said a female voice. Only then did Brand see that, in the corpse's wiry black fingers, it grasped the Idol of the Great Mother, and that the idol's golden lips were moving.

A sense of dread fell over Brand, but he forced himself out of its control. "I came to speak to the High King," Brand said. "Not a demon."

"I am not a demon," the Great Mother said. "I am of this mortal world like you. Your customs are different from mine and that of my people. But in your arrogance—in your unwavering belief that you are right and good—you humans came to my land, and drove out my people, and destroyed my shrines." With a crack, the idol broke out of the corpse's fingers and floated up into the air. "Now—even if I cannot fully bring my people back—I can rain death upon you through my daughter... I can bring back the trolls to the Ice Shelf and have them rebuild my Grand Shrine."

Brand removed his cloak and drew his sword. Harald followed.

"A fight is what you want?" the idol said. "Is it a fight really what you need, boy?" Its little golden arm stretched outward. "Arise, champion!"

With a crack, the corpse stood up.

"None have dared oppose the High King," the idol said. "I have appointed him Sovereign of Badelgard, and even Lord Sigmund Blackhelm has dared not steal the throne."

"Then Sigmund is a traitor to goodness!" Harald said.

Brand threw his cloak at the idol. It missed and drifted to the tile floor.

Harald stepped toward the corpse. "By the customs of our forebears... I, Harald Riverhall, challenge you, Sven Oster and High King, to a duel," he said and drew out his ancestral sword. "We duel to death."

A shimmering blade appeared in dead Sven's decrepit hand. It was curved, unlike those of Badelgard warriors, and forged with ornamental markings; it was an Ulfr blade like Brand had sometimes seen on display in marketplaces.

The corpse-king cut with its blade and Harald parried narrowly. It stepped forward and hacked down, and Harald just barely deflected the blow.

Brand picked up his cloak, leapt, and tossed again. It fell around the idol, which crashed to the ground. Brand wrapped it tight as a loud, shrill scream issued from its mouth. Due to the power contained within, his heart was pounding out of control. His breath turned to short, shrill rasps.

"I must... I must go!" Brand said.

"Why must you go?" Harald demanded as he knocked aside another quick cut. "Do not betray the House Riverhall!"

But Brand was already running away, the woolen cloak fluttering the idol's high pitched screams echoing through the winter air.

Down in the low-town was a blacksmith. Once, while Brand was studying at the Skalds' College, Gunnar worked there. Now, he was coming to old Hennard with an altogether different request: a request which the old man never had before, and which Gunnar—bless his soul—never had the misfortune of doing.

The Idol of the Great Mother kept screaming. "Let me go! Let me go at once!" it said, and did not shut up when Brand struck it and or whispered blasphemies to the Great Mother. The Oskir citizens gawked at him as he lumbered down the steep steps to the low-town.

At last he reached the shore of the river that led into King's Falls. He reached the blacksmith a few seconds later, and saw that Hennard was working at something, pounding away with his hammer. When the shrill screeching of the idol reached his ears, he looked up at Brand.

"Dear Hennard!" Brand shouted as loudly as he could. "You are a good man! Please, melt this idol down into gold."

The screaming reached a pinnacle and Brand's ears began to throb in pain at the volume. He could hear nothing but the screaming sound of the idol.

Hennard's mouth formed the words, "What?"

Brand tossed the idol into the flames of the forge. Little by little, as the gold melted away, the screaming faded; until finally, there was no sound but the rushing wind and the thunderous pounding of Brand's own heart.

Brand raced back to the Golden House as fast as his legs could carry him.

When he got to the throne room Lady Alysse was crying as she stooped over Harald's bloodied body. He had taken a puncture wound deep in the chest. Blood was spreading across the wooden floor.

A few inches from him, a crown sat amid a pile of black ash. That was all that remained of the High King: his greedy crown of gold, and his blackened remains. It was the end of his life, and all he had to show for it.

"Curses!" Alysse said, choked with tears, as she knelt over the corpse of Harald. "Curses have fallen upon me and the Line of Riverhall. But death was the punishment of the High King! That honorless, evil scum just vanished… burst into a pile of black dust, but not before he murdered my husband."

Brand knelt beside her and put a reassuring hand on her shoulder. "It will be all right."

"I never bore him a child," Alysse said. "I never even was intimate… and yet… I loved him, and admired him more than words can express." She kept crying. "Will he turn into one of them? The darklings? Like that woman you invited to our hall?"

"I don't think so," Brand said. With the power of the idol gone, perhaps her dark curse over Badelgard had lifted. "And even if he does die, we must give him a proper burial," he added.

"In the cemetery outside Oskir," Alysse said, "where all the noble warrior-men are buried."

She picked up the crown that the corpse once wore and placed it on Brand's head. Never—not in a thousand lifetimes—did Brand think he'd wear the jeweled gold-and-velvet crown of the High King. It was utmost dishonor to do so. A lowborn would never have a claim to the throne, not even if he were made a housecarl. Brand laughed.

"It looks good on you," Alysse said. "Perhaps you are of noble birth."

"I am not, I assure you," Brand said. "My friend Gunnar was, even though they called him 'Whoreson.' Magnus Blackhelm was his father. I am just Brand son of Gutlaff, a swineherd; and I am happy with that."

"You are housecarl now," Alysse said. "My housecarl and the father of the Riverhalls. I regret that marrying you is not possible, love. But when our noble house is reestablished, you are welcome to it at any time, in any state of health or mind."

"That means everything to me," Brand said as he picked the

crown off his head.

He cast the cruel object onto the floor.

The next day they placed Harald's body in a coffin and began an all-day procession to the Church of Vana. The stone church had windows of colored glass that depicted mountain peaks, warrior-maidens, harps and other things sacred to the goddess of victory. At the double doors, two towering statues of valkyrie warriors stood guard with stone spears. The people of Oskir, dressed in peasant browns and grays, gathered to watch the nobleman die. They did not know Harald as Brand knew him—a strange man, and a luxuriant man, but perhaps one of honor. Honor, because without his diversion, a corpse would still sit on the throne and the Great Mother's eye would still be over Badelgard.

Alysse followed the procession sadly, dry-eyed because there were no more tears to be shed. Brand did cry a little, though it was unfitting for a man. Funerals always made him cry; he was a housecarl, now, but a sensitive musician at heart.

At the end of the procession, the gray skies opened up, and a drizzle began. There was winter rain in Oskir sometimes, but after prior events, Brand had thought it would never rain again.

Tidings turned for the worse almost immediately after the funeral. Someone came with the news that the Wildsaber clan and the Blackhelm clan—acting in unison—were riding to Oskir to put Sigmund Blackhelm on the High King's throne.

Captain Erik and the River Guard stood watch outside the Riverhall baronial longhouse while Sir Brand shivered and bit his fingers in fear. "We should go," he said. "I don't think the Wildsabers like me. You, they don't mind as much; but Kenna does not like me… she does not like me being a housecarl. Not at all."

"Kenna is a she-wolf, and that's putting it nicely," Alysse said.

"Like a she-wolf, she must be hunted to protect the herd: the people of Badelgard."

"That is poetic," Brand said. "Perhaps you should be a skald and not me."

"Lies," Alysse said, and hugged him tight. "You are the poet and musician. You are the bringer of joy and mirth, and the bringer of fear and contemplation." She buried her nose in his kirtle. "Oh, how I love you, Brand."

"And I you," Brand answered her. "And I you."

At dusk they came: a thousand men, riding through the Golden Gate on warhorses like a battalion of hell. Lord Sigmund Blackhelm—his hair the flame red of his father, Magnus—rode at the fore, girt in chainmail and carrying a greathelm in his huge hands.

Brand watched from a high perch. He watched as they poured through the gate. Further back in the host was Kenna Wildsaber, riding on a white horse; and her girls behind her, riding on ponies. Stenn was not there; it served her right, and, in truth, it served Stenn right too.

"I should not dishonor the dead with insults," Brand told himself, and sprinted back to the Riverhall guesthouse.

It was only a matter of minutes before the host had gathered together outside the Golden House. And it was only an hour before Brand's bad feeling was proven true; a host of a hundred mounted warriors, plus Lady Kenna, rode up to the Riverhall guesthouse. The only thing protecting Alysse and Brand was a line of twelve River Guards blocking the door.

"Do you wish to arrest us?" Alysse asked, standing in the Guard's shadow. "If so, what are you terms? Speak, she-wolf; or can you only bark and bite?"

Kenna's eyes narrowed. "I will only speak to the lord of the household."

"Harald is dead," Alysse said. "And you have no right to arrest me."

Kenna smiled. "If Sigmund Blackhelm is High King and vests me with authority," she said as a dark smile crept over her features, "then I can do anything I want and you have no choice but to listen."

"And has he vested you with authority?" Alysse asked.

Kenna's smile faded slightly. "He wants to speak with you and Brand so that you may tell him what happened to the High King."

Lord Sigmund Blackhelm, earl of Trowheim, sat in the throne with the High King's Crown on his lap. "Tell me, boy, what has happened to Sven."

Brand stood with Alysse before the throne without the River Guard, at the total mercy of Sigmund's soldiers.

"Sigmund," Brand said, choosing not to address him by the proper title, "Do not call me a boy. I am a man and have seen much evil in my time."

The sharp, stinging pain of a lash hit Brand. He yelped and recoiled. He looked back and realized that Sigmund's torturers, wearing black masks and black robes, stood behind him; and hooked to their belts were more instruments than just whips: clippers, thumbscrews, and more. It was no matter.

"I repeat myself," Sigmund said. "Tell me, boy, what has happened to the High King."

"I am not a boy," Brand said.

The pain was sharper this time, and more acute; and there was a loud cracking sound as the whip dug into flesh. But this time, Brand didn't yelp.

Sigmund's expression grew stern. "Tell me—"

"Sir Brand!" Alysse hissed.

Sigmund glared at her, then looked back to Brand and said,

"What happened to the High King?"

Brand pointed to the pile of black powder on the ground. "By the time I got to Oskir with the Riverhalls, he was not Sven anymore. By the time I had ridden to Oskir, he had turned to a demon. He was possessed by the Idol of the Great Mother. I melted it in the forge, and he collapsed."

"He called the High King a demon!" Kenna's voice said from behind.

Alysse looked back and hissed, "Shut it, she-wolf."

"Quiet!" Sigmund roared.

The whips cut into Alysse's dress and she fell to her knees with a sharp cry.

Sigmund looked intensely at Brand. "The king's attendants tell me that you brought that idol to him," he said. "Is this true?"

"Yes," Brand said.

Alysse looked up at him, apparently in disbelief at his foolish honesty. The whips struck him again, and tears of pain formed in his eyes; yet, he did not buckle under.

"Have you not, therefore, committed treason against the High King?" Sigmund said.

"Call it what you will," Brand said. "He asked for the idol, and I gave it to him."

Sigmund frowned. "Let him be hanged."

"He is lowborn!" Lady Kenna shrieked. "He must be tortured first."

Alysse stood up and turned around, fiery-eyed with anger. "Sir Brand is my housecarl. He is, therefore, not lowborn. He will not be tortured, and—by the Green Dragon—" She turned around to face Sigmund. "Do not let him be executed. He does not deserve it." She fell to her knees and knit her fingers together. "I beg of you, Sigmund. If there is any goodness in that heart of yours, please let Brand live. He does not deserve to die. He is a good man; and an honest man, and he said he did as the king asked."

"You have moved me, woman," Sigmund said. "And I will compromise."

"Thank you, milord," Brand said.

"He will still be executed," Sigmund said.

Brand gasped and his heart shuddered.

"However," Sigmund said, "As housecarl, he will not face torture. He is not lowborn as Lady Kenna says. He will be hanged tomorrow at sundown."

"And what about the southern whore?" hissed Lady Kenna.

"Seeing she and her husband have parted ways, I strip her of her noble titles," Sigmund said, "and I exile her from Badelgard. She has a month to leave, and—as the new High King—I will lower the Drawbridge enough for her proper exit."

CHAPTER TWENTY-TWO

They were hanging two people today, and had two nooses tied on two platforms. Brand prayed to the gods silently, asking that the good Lady Vana would grant him rest, and, above all, entry into the Hall of the Slain. At a younger age, he would have asked for revenge; but he had learned that vengeance takes care of itself, and the evil ones always destroy themselves. At least, that was how things were in songs and ballads.

The hangman was addressing a large crowd of lowborns—like a sea of gray and brown—that had gathered to watch the execution. "One of these dying today is a traitor to the High King and to his sovereign realm. His actions led to the poisoning of the king's soul; his transformation into a monstrosity; and, in time, his death. Let this be a lesson to all of you! No man may cross the High King and live. And now that Sigmund is High King of Badelgard, let it be clear to one and all that any who cross him will have a similar fate, and—for the lowborns—far worse. These two are highborn—"

Brand took no pride in that.

"—and they will not be put on the rack or tortured like any of you would be if you crossed the High King." He paused. "This other criminal dying here today has committed offenses which can hardly be read in public; yet the king wishes to do it anyway. It is a woman. She has murdered. She has whored. She has stolen valuable items that did not belong to her. She has worn men's clothing."

There were a few giggles in the crowd.

"And in recent times, she has forcibly castrated a servant of the Frostfall earl."

The crowd howled with laughter, and Brand joined them, chuckling despite his fate. He knew beyond a doubt who this woman was; the most wonderful, and the most notorious woman-thief Badelgard had ever seen, and, perhaps, would ever see again.

"It is not funny!" the hangman shouted.

But the crowd kept laughing.

The attendants shoved Brand up the stairs, onto the platform. A familiar face was just a yard away from him.

"Hilda!" he said.

"Brand!" she said, and smiled.

As the executioner shouted on about the penalties for committing crimes, they had a whispered conversation.

"I thought they would execute you," Brand said.

"The darklings attacked us; I fought them off, and then I killed all Jannik's guards and left him with a… decisive… wound."

"You have more a sense of justice than Sigmund," Brand said.

"And you are housecarl?" Hilda said.

Brand nodded. Hilda smiled.

"Stop talking!" barked an attendant, who then jerked a noose around Brand's neck. Another attendant did the same with Hilda.

"You are a good man, Brand," Hilda said. "No longer will I call you a boy."

Brand smiled.

An attendant slapped Hilda hard across the cheek for talking, and she spat in his face. He slapped her again, and she spat again. Finally, the attendant gave up and, together with the other, left the platform.

"We bring you here two villains," the hangman said. "Let them be a lesson to you all."

The hangman walked over to Brand and jerked a black sack over his head. He could no longer see. The hangman walked over to Hilda and doubtlessly did the very same thing.

"Brand, son of Gutlaff, do you have any last words?"

"Throw that crown in the mud, Sigmund Whoreson, because it doesn't belong to you!" Brand cried. "And go eat the flesh of babes, Kenna, she-wolf! I can't wait until the hunter finally puts an arrow in your neck."

The crowd roared and clapped.

The hangman scoffed. "Cheer again, lowborn scum," he

screamed, "and we will slaughter all of you like a herd of swine!"

The cheering died down and the hangman asked Hilda to give her last words.

"Brand," she called out, "many would call this a black day—a day of gloomy skies, and frost, and snow. But I say, rejoice! For tonight, we feast with Gunnar in Altgard!"

The last thing Brand felt in the material world was the platform giving out beneath his feet.

Cloaked in the gray, hooded robe of a lowborn, Alysse watched as Brand fell to the hangman's noose. Eyes filled with tears of rage, she reflected and she plotted. They may have killed Brand, and that woman-friend of his which—gods knew—she had tried to save. They may have killed the hero who put an end to the power of the dark idol. And yet, there were still things left to be done. Alysse was not the kind of woman who easily forgave. She was a woman who hated and fought injustice and, above all, held grudges.

I'll go back to Zarubain. I'll bring back an army of a thousand knights. That is what she had wanted to say yesterday to threaten Lord Sigmund as he handed down his pronouncement; but now that it had come to this, she was glad Sigmund didn't know of her plans.

She walked slowly away, down the shoveled path to Oskir. In a few weeks, she'd walk down the King's Drawbridge. But by Vana, and by the Green Dragon, and—gods!—by the ghost of Sir Brand, this was just the beginning. She would have her revenge upon these petty warrior-nobles. No backward Badelgard nobleman could stand against a duke's daughter.

She knew one thing above all else: the child stirring inside her would be High King.

Book Two, High Queen, is available now.

HIGH QUEEN PREVIEW

CHAPTER ONE:
Kai Riverhall

The little girl stumbled toward Kai Riverhall, her eyes glassy and frozen, her lips rimmed with dried blood. She was a darkling, but even battle-hardened Kai found it difficult to strike down someone who was—or once had been—so young.

"Don't kill me," she whispered without moving her lips. "Please?"

Kai gulped.

"Stay still," said the darkling girl. "Just… let me touch you."

Kai released the bowstring. The arrow flew forward and pierced her icy, frozen forehead. She shrieked and fell to the ground. Darklings could only be killed via a blow to the head. Sword, club, arrow—it didn't matter what weapon, as long as you hit in the right spot.

This was Kai's first kill of the day, but it almost certainly would not be his last. The darklings wandered the forest in increasing numbers. Scoutmaster Frey wanted every one of his underlings to kill at least ten daily. Lately, the darklings hadn't retreated into shadows at day; it seemed they were now immune to the rays of the sun.

Kai walked up to the corpse and stooped down. The girl wore a soft white dress—silk, it looked like. Once, she was a rich girl; perhaps even related to the Riverhalls.

Kai was a Riverhall too. Ha! He had no silk clothing. Being a Riverhall did not mean that you were rich, at least not in the Order of Scouts. He drew back his hand before he could touch her skin.

Do not touch the darklings, Frey had said. *Do not touch them, or anything they carry.*

Kai wandered through the forest, silent as a lynx, waiting for a darkling to pop out at any moment. One of them had wounded his fellow scout, Uthrik; Scoutmaster Frey had to decapitate him with a sword. Kai did not want to repeat Uthrik's fate.

Rustling began above, up a steep ridge. Kai backed away and fitted an arrow to his string. There was something in the leafy green up above—a presence that made Kai's neck-hairs stand on end and a chill pass through his body.

Something grunted. Then, rustling began in the ferns. Heavy, trudging footsteps echoed through the air. The gait of the creature— whoever it was—was slow and confused. It had two feet—Kai could tell that much—and it was not a deer or a lynx. Could it be a bear? The footsteps certainly sounded heavy enough.

A lump grew in Kai's throat. "Who are you?" he whimpered.

"*Sio Soreldi,*" a voice said.

Kai gulped. "Pardon?"

"*Cani Orion. Miuru.*"

The scent of rot, earth, and the juices of the grave filled Kai's nostrils. He looked up at the cliff inquisitively. The creature was close now.

Kai shuddered and his fingers trembled. The arrow loosed of its own accord. It soared through the air and hit a tree. Kai thought of running. The creature's footsteps indicated it was close, now.

He looked up at the cliff. What came next, he didn't remember.

The triangular pinewood ceiling of Woodhome stretched above him, and the burning logs of a hearth-fire bathed him in light. The moose heads and deer heads hung along the log walls. Kai was at home.

"He's not moving," said the voice of Scoutmaster Frey. The man's long golden hair dangled below his shoulders. His brown eyes scanned up and down Kai's body.

"I found him in the Ninth Ward," said Helgun, Kai's best friend, as he stepped into view.

Frey ran his coarse woodsman's fingers across Kai's arms. "Do you remember what happened? What did you see?"

Kai described what he had heard. He described the terror he had felt, but he remembered nothing more. "Looking back, I think I sensed a creeping power from him. Some kind of aura, but it was dark... evil..."

"You remember nothing," Frey said. "What you did see you have forgotten. Witchcraft, indeed."

Kai turned his head and looked around. Everything stood in its proper place: the orange log walls, the brown bearskin rugs, and the antlered heads of stags on the walls. Yet he did not feel altogether well. "I wonder if I'll ever remember what happened."

"Trust and believe," said Master Frey. "Then, perhaps."

"He told me '*Sio Soreldi*' and '*Cani Orion. M—*'"

Frey hushed him. "Stay your tongue," he snapped. "Do not speak the language of the Ulfr."

Kai raised a brow. "The words are in the Ulfr language?"

"They sound like it."

"If it is the Ulfr tongue, we can send for a lexicon," Kai answered. "We can go to Oskir—"

"The king will not let us borrow such a valuable book," Master Frey answered. "You know this as well as I. Besides, Oskir is far... "

"We can go to the library ourselves," Kai said. "Surely the darklings have no interest in books or learning."

"I will hear no more of it," Frey dismissed him. "Now relax the rest of the night." He walked away into the distance.

Kai tried to ease himself off the table. His muscles were tight, as stiff as the statues of Riverhall Forest. After a struggle he got moving again.

The next day, just as always, Kai went out on patrol. His muscles ached, and a headache clouded all thought. The fact that Frey assigned him the Twelfth Ward only partially explained his pains. The Twelfth Ward comprised the north-eastern section of the Great Wood that bordered the ghost town of Andarr's Port. Though it used to be the safest, now the scouts dreaded patrolling it.

Despite the aches, he continued on and tried his best to hide his discomfort. The Scouts of Woodhome valued bravery, overcoming pain, and manliness above all other virtues. Harald, the baron and Kai's distant relation, did not believe in such virtues; and the Order of Scouts found it difficult to respect him.

An entire darkling family came into view: a man, a woman, and three toddling children. Their curse had turned their skin a pale, frosty hue and their eyes hard as icicles. Kai loosed five arrows in quick sequence and struck each one in the head. These were the slow darklings, the "shamblers." The living dead varied in strength, with shamblers as the weakest.

At about noon, Kai's wanderings took him to the edge of Andarr's Port. The sheer silence never failed to surprise him. In the past, when Kai patrolled the Twelfth Ward, the city's noise overwhelmed his senses. Now, on this cool summer day, the only sounds were the pitter-patter of rain and the wind howling through the empty buildings.

A shrill, panicked scream resounded through the air: a woman's scream.

Darklings don't sound like that.

He followed the scream to its source and found a woman—a rich woman, judging by her scarlet-dyed satin dress and jeweled golden necklaces. A large white stallion nickered nervously a few feet away.

A darkling crouched before the woman, fangs bared and claws extended. It had no right arm; only a frozen stump remained. Kai quietly circled the darkling, not wanting to scare it into attacking the woman. But he needed to shoot from a less dangerous angle.

At last, he pulled back his bow and released the bowstring. In an instant the arrow was through the darkling's head, and the monster fell to the ground.

The woman seemed more shocked at the explosion than grateful to Kai. Still, Kai made his way over to her. He trod slowly, making sure not to frighten her further.

"Milady?" Kai said in as gentlemanly a tone as he could muster.

"I heard the rumors about Andarr's Port, that it is a ghost town," the woman said, her brown eyes looking away from Kai as if he wasn't there. "I didn't think the darklings came out by day."

"Their power has grown, milady," Kai said. "Perhaps you should head east for safety."

"I am looking for my son," the woman said. "He has turned into one of *them*, but I know that if he looks into his mother's eyes, he will change back to normal."

"I advise against that, milady," Kai said. "The darklings cannot change back. Not even a mother's love can change them back."

"Do not call me a fool!" the woman snapped. "What is your station, boy?"

"I am highborn," Kai answered. "I am a Riverhall."

"Harald Riverhall is dead, and his wife Alysse has been exiled, never to return," the woman said. "The Line of Riverhall is vanquished. Only my son—the one I must reclaim—is a Riverhall. He is the last male Riverhall alive, but I, Kenna, will make him a proper Wildsaber."

Impossible. Kai looked at her closely. Her eyes seemed truthful. "What is a proper lady doing without a full guard?"

"They were eaten—" Kenna stopped whatever she was about to say. "I do not need to speak to you, Riverhall. I must find my son"

"Your son is gone, milady. He is not coming back."

"You don't know that," Kenna hissed. "My poor Stenn *will* come back to me. And I will find him."

"Suit yourself," Kai said, then turned and headed back toward the center of the forest—the First Ward, where Woodhome lay—to tell Scoutmaster Frey of the demise of Lord Harald and Lady Alysse.

CHAPTER TWO:
Alysse Riverhall

Things had not changed much in the kingdom of Zarubain. That was Alysse's first impression as she stepped off the riverboat and entered her father's land, the duchy of Voraigne. The boughs of the hemlocks and firs dripped with recent rain. Despite the wetness, warmth permeated the air. Alysse was warmer than she'd been in decades and for a brief second she wondered whether she might never return to Badelgard, but she cast that thought aside immediately. Her desire to set things right by far outweighed her desire for comfort.

Her father, Ergould Vis Voraigne, lived in a vast manor on a quiet lake. Vast compared to Riverhall Castle; not 'vast' compared to the manors of other dukes. It was not built specifically for comfort like Riverhall Castle; Voraigne Manor had tall stone walls, battlements, a moat, and a drawbridge. War between the kings' subjects was common in Zarubain, more common than it was in Badelgard; at least, more common than it currently was in Badelgard. Gods knew the earls used to fight with equal ferocity until the Oster dynasty came into control.

Jays, river thrushes and robins flitted through the moist evergreen forest, singing their beautiful songs. In Zarubain, Alysse had been taught that invisible fairies lived under the ponds and in the weeds and on the boughs of the trees, but she never believed it. Her father's fairy-priestess never impressed Alysse with her intelligence, even though Madame Flourelle had been taught at the Lady's Cathedral in Zarubad.

The manor appeared in view, a towering castle of dark gray against the almost-blinding greenness of the forest. It felt so strange to come back after so many years. What awaited her here? What had happened to her father, the honorable duke Ergould? Most importantly, what had happened to the House Vis Voraigne?

She crossed the distance to the castle. Mallards swam in the family lake. Paddling through the lily-covered water on a rowboat was her father. Age had turned his hair gray and his skin wrinkled. He still wore nice clothing: a fine purple tunic and woolen breeches, so very unlike the thick kirtles of Badelgard. Gold rings gleamed on his fingers and a glittering diamond brooch held his cloak together.

"Father!" Alysse cried, dropping her luggage.

Her father looked up at her. "My dear," he said, and began paddling toward her. Eventually he reached the shore and hauled himself onto the moist forest floor, each step obviously painful. "My dear Alysse… I was sure that I would never see you again."

"Father," she said, "it is so good to see you."

They embraced. "Alysse vis Voraigne," he said.

"Alysse Riverhall," she corrected him. "I will never change my name. I love Harald so, even though he is dead."

"Surely not!" Ergould cried. "He is too young to die. Was it illness?"

"He died in war, father," Alysse said. "The king of Badelgard murdered him. Then I was exiled."

Ergould gasped. "Those smelly, barbaric northmen! How dare they treat a woman of Vis Voraigne stock like that? It is criminal, I tell you… criminal! But now you can come back; live with me, and when your younger brother inherits the duchy you will live the rest of your life in comfort. It is not so bad."

"Father," Alysse said, "I have lived away from home too long. I have lived under Harald's protection too long. I am a daughter of Badelgard now…"

"Nonsense," said Ergould. "Our fortunes are increased. We own twice the land than when you left. Besides… once you have Zarube cuisine tonight, you won't be able to leave."

The fried snails, the sour crab roasts, the cheese-stuffed duckling and the fermented cow tongues brought memories back to Alysse, but that was all they did. Too long had Alysse feasted on the mead, the roast pork and the crispy potatoes of Badelgard. She no longer preferred the high cuisine of the Zarube king's court. In fact, it tasted strange to her, though she'd never tell her father that; insulting the king's culinary preferences was social suicide.

Her father devoured the fermented cow tongues, one after another. He had grown slightly plumper since Alysse had last seen him; nothing to worry about, but it was easy to see that he had chosen the relaxed life in his old age.

"Where is my brother?" Alysse said, glancing at a plate of butter-fried lamb eyes in distaste.

"Your brother Lourges is at war," said Ergould. "He has taken an army south into a petty count's lands and will be back by week's end. The duchy is expanding at a lynx's pace… and one day, even the Golden Lion of the king will not be able to stand against the Red Hawk."

For some reason, Alysse doubted that the king's standard would ever fall to the Vis Voraignes. "My dear father—one who gave me life— I must be honest with you. I need knights. I need soldiers. I need an army to take back Badelgard."

"Why does a woman need an army?" Ergould said.

"Not even in Zarubain—not even in the bloody *southlands*—can I escape woman-hatred!" Alysse glared at her father.

"I apologize, my dear," Ergould said. "I should not speak like one of the northmen. I simply do not understand why you won't stay here."

"I desire to return to my adopted home," Alysse said. "It has become a part of me, like an arm or a leg."

"Then we must cut it off," Ergould said. "The living in Zarubain is good. Wealth is plentiful, save for the dirty peasants. And the food—"

"I hate the food!" Alysse snapped. She had finally gathered the gumption. "I am sick of lamb's eyes, and boiled snail, and fermented cabbage. Don't you understand, father? I want an army more than anything. I need it."

"You cannot just come here, ask for an army, and leave!"

Ergould said. "Think of your father! Think of your old, sickly father who has been so worried about his daughter. You have never written to me, Alysse. And now you show up in my twilight years and ask for an army."

"Father, I love you; and that's why you must do this," Alysse said.

Her statement contained a grain of truth. In some ways, she did love her father. In others she did not. He had sent her off at the age of fourteen to be married to a blasted northman. He hadn't listened to her tears as she begged him to let her stay home. He had told her, "You must do this for the sake of our line!" and "Have some respect for your family!" and finally, "I don't care about what you want!" That was why she hadn't written to him. Because Alysse held grudges. She held one of the biggest against her father because—even though Harald had turned out to be a good man and not much older than her—Ergould hadn't cared about what she wanted.

She did love her distant, uncaring father in some ways, because it was every daughter's duty to love her father if he did not abuse her. And Ergould hadn't abused her in any obvious way; only ignored her feelings, wants, and desires. Only ignored her. Only used her as a political tool.

"My daughter, you look angry," Ergould said. "I am sorry if I have offended you."

"No, you haven't," Alysse said. She reached out and touched his wrinkled old hand. "And if I was, I wasn't for long. I just wish you'd understand... I need to go back to Badelgard. A woman has slighted me... killed my husband... killed my dear friend and musician. Surely you can understand my wrath."

Ergould's expression softened. "I can," he said.

The rain picked up again in the evening. It was a cooling, misty rain. Alysse sat in her old bed with its feather-stuffed mattress and its purple drapes and looked outside the window into the yard, into the forest of firs and hemlocks. It was the ducal wood, set aside for the

Master of the House Vis Voraigne. Just a mile away, the peasants' farms began.

The lowborn did not fare well in Badelgard, but in Zarubain they fared even worse. How many times, as a girl, had Alysse seen their wretchedness: their filthy hovels; their backbreaking work; their mangy, thin forms? And how much had Alysse taken for granted her high and lofty position, her life of comfort and plentiful food? It was not the duty of a noble to have pity on the poor, but Alysse felt for them anyway. They were pitiful and wretched, but they were people too; only people that had no luck.

She looked out the forest once again—a brilliantly green scene of moss-draped evergreens. She wondered if her brother would ever come back for war.

He did come back one stormy night, a week later. Outside, lightning flashed and thunder rolled through the ducal wood. At first, when there was a loud knocking on the door, Alysse thought it was just a series of harsh lightning-bolts. But her father got up from the table—they were having an unfortunate dinner of bread and duck-liver pate—and Alysse followed.

The door swung open before they reached it. A shadowy figure stood in the open doorway, dressed in a knee-length hauberk. He was pale and looked deathly tired. Alysse had never seen him as an adult, only as a child; when Alysse left at age fourteen, Lourges was only seven.

And what a tall, handsome man he had become, despite the effects of his obvious fatigue. His eyes were green like Alysse; he had an even face, a prominent jaw, and a button nose; and topping it all was a thick set of blond hair, held up by a headband.

"My brother!" Alysse cried.

"My sister," Lourges said, somewhat less emphatically. "I have not seen you for an age. If only you could see me in victory, and not in defeat."

"What do you mean?" Ergould said in an accusatory tone.

"The count of Garrone has routed our troops. He is a brilliant general, my father. I have disappointed you and brought shame to our noble house."

"How many men?" Ergould growled.

"Pardon?" Lourges said.

"*How many men?*" Ergould hissed.

"Two hundred common footmen have been killed. Sir Arcibaud, Sir Jierreau and Sir Jacouie have died and gone to see the gods, but fifty proper knights remain," Lourges said. "In all, it was not a bad loss; but any loss is a shame."

"It is a crime against nature for the House Vis Voraigne to lose against *anyone!*" Ergould shouted.

"I am sorry, father," Lourges said.

"Who commanded the retreat?" Ergould said. "If you still had some seven thousand footmen left, why did you not keep fighting?"

Indeed, Alysse thought. *Only a coward would retreat with those numbers.*

"Well," Lourges said, obviously not wanting to tell the truth. "The army was large, and Sir Jourmande—"

"Sir Jourmande is *not* the commanding field-marshal," Ergould said. "You are the leader of my army."

"They will not listen to me… they only listen to Sir Jourmande."

Then you are an even greater coward than I believed, Alysse thought.

"You are a wretch," Ergould said. "Now come and have some duck-liver pate. Actually, forget it; you may only eat bread as punishment."

Lourges' embarrassment was great, but the conversation eventually turned to gentler topics. He asked if Alysse was with child.

"I am. My husband has died," Alysse said, and then, knowing she had to lie about the proper paternity, added, "But Harald has left me with a gift. A child is inside me, waiting to be born."

Lourges smiled weakly, despite the obvious shame written on his features. "If only he is half as strong as you… and as beautiful. Perhaps he will be."

"I am neither strong, nor am I particularly beautiful," Alysse said. "But thank you, brother." She forced down a bite of pate-smeared bread and washed it down with wine—a drink she only rarely enjoyed in Badelgard. She hesitated a second, wondering it was the proper time, and then finally spoke her mind. "These petty wars are not worth the army Vis Voraigne."

"How do you mean, sister?" said Lourges.

"The land of Badelgard is there for the taking," Alysse continued, carefully measuring the expression on Lourges' face and adjusting her tone properly. "With my help—as a Riverhall who is a legitimate contender to the throne by marriage—you could annex the land, and Badelgard could belong to our noble house."

Lourges laughed. "The northmen are smelly, dirty, and poor… barbarians at their cores. What interest would I have in them?"

"There is plentiful wealth there," Alysse said. "Iron mines, copper mines… furs, antlers, and endless timber… men and women fit—nay, *happy*—at the prospect of servitude." Alysse hated lying, but it was necessary. No Badelgard lowborn would happily enter into Zarube-style servitude.

"Pray tell, sister," Lourges said, "why you are here and not in Andarr's Port with your family?"

"The family is dead. Harald is dead. My skald is dead. A she-wolf, Lady Kenna, has slain them all." Alysse's cheeks grew flushed with anger. "Tell me, brother, how many men are under your command?"

"My dear sister," Lourges said, his voice dripping with derision, "I cannot agree to come with you and fight under the Riverhall banner. Your request is foolish, and borders on childlike. Have I not mentioned our house is in peril?"

Alysse's anger diverted from Lady Kenna and focused on her brother. "It is only in peril because you are a cowa—" She caught herself. "—because your friend made a command to retreat."

"Do not talk to me in such a manner, sister," Lourges said. "You have asked for an answer and I have given it: a firm, resounding 'No.' If you intend to go back to Badelgard, you came here for naught. Your husband has died, and now you must return to our home—under your father's care, under my care."

"I will not be resigned to a prison," Alysse said. "I am free to make my own decisions and you have no say in them."

"Suit yourself," Lourges said, and a dark smile crept over his features. "But you won't be getting an army."

Alysse would see about that. Her brother lacked the courage and manhood to command his own troops; and Alysse was not discouraged easily.

GLOSSARY

Altgard: See Hall of the Slain.

Buntringer: The ancestor of the Badelgard people. His sons were Hjarta, Himnall, and Helgur, from whom the human population of Badelgard descends.

Dragonmount, the: A tall peak in the northeast of Badelgard where the Green Dragon once slumbered. The ancient Ulfr believed it was haunted and knew that a great beast slept there, but dared not disturb it.

Green Dragon, the: The dragon, named Skruga, who allied with the Badelgard humans and destroyed the ancient Ulfr with fire. He is believed to be the last dragon to leave for the west.

Green Dragons: The priesthood of Skruga residing in a stone temple at the base of the Dragonmount.

Half-Breeds: A population of mixed human and elven lineage that lives north of Badelgard and around the shore of the Inner Sea.

Hall of the Slain: Also known as Altgard, this is the place where Vana, goddess of victory, and her valkyries are supposed to reside. It is believed to be a spacious longhouse in a mountain meadow within the broader realm of heaven. Only skilled warriors and men of great honor are chosen to live in the presence of Lady Vana and her warrior-maidens. By day, the risen dead fight, but at night, they recover from any wounds they received during the day and feast until the early hours of the morning in the presence of the valkyries.

Horse Chiefs: The Badelgard term for the Murghul people. The Murghuli are nomads but frequently visit the area southeast of the Sky Cliffs, which is a great hunting ground. Because of their proximity to the King's Drawbridge, they have come into frequent contact with Badelgarders in the past. The Badelgarders consider them dishonorable because they use hit-and-run archery tactics as their primary means of combat. In faith, the

Murghuli revere Eliane—horse goddess—whose worship has spread to Badelgard.

Housecarl: An order of protectors for the various noble houses. Housecarls are considered highborn and are required to defend their lieges to the death if need be. Appointment to housecarl is the only way a lowborn can enter the nobility. A housecarl can be stripped of his rank easily; all it requires is the liege-lord's verbal pronouncement. The order is open to both men and women.

King's Drawbridge, the: An enormous wooden drawbridge that can only be lowered via the High King's command. It is the only way, excluding sea travel, that a person can enter the low-lying southern lands. In winter, it is Badelgard's sole exit. High King Sven has not lowered it since the beginning of his reign.

Nobility: The nobility of Badelgard is called highborn and expected to rule above the common, or lowborn. At heart they are a warrior class, and in their inception expected to protect the kingdom and shy away from any temptations of luxury or excess. The top tier of the nobility consists of the earls, who rule great towns and citadels across Badelgard. Below earls are the barons. Only one baronial family owns land and rules its own city: the Riverhalls of Andarr's Port. The other barons rule petty villages. The Osters, an earl family, took the High Throne after the Accession Crisis of 656 and changed the name of the capital from Rigthorp to Oskir.

River Guard: An ancient order of soldiers dedicated to protecting the Line of Riverhall. They serve as bodyguards to the baronial family and are sworn to do whatever the lord baron wishes, no matter how outrageous the command.

Skalds' College: An academy in Oskir where skalds—or professional musicians—are trained. The college is the only of its kind in Badelgard, and its graduates can be found in earls' courts all across the nation. Other skalds choose to bond themselves to adventuring warriors and compose songs of their deeds.

Skruga: See Green Dragon.

Sky Cliffs, the: A sheer precipice separating Badelgard from the low-lying southern lands. They stretch approximately 2,000 feet and can only be descended via the King's Drawbridge.

Troll: A large, hulking creation of Ulfr wizards. No human alive has seen a troll.

Ulfr: A human term for the people that originally inhabited Badelgard. The Ulfr called themselves the Sorelden, and called their land Sorelda. As a people, the Ulfr had many customs that the human invaders thought to be odd or even evil. They suffered the effects of severe inbreeding due to widespread brother-sister marriages, which caused a number of physical deformities: instead of five toes, most Sorelden had two large toes; only three fingers and a thumb on each hand; and yellow eyes. They worshiped a deity called The Great Mother whom the invading humans identified as a demon. Each year, there was a lottery and those Ulfr families who were picked had to sacrifice one of their children to The Great Mother. Despite their deformities, the Ulfr were powerful wizards and most of them—perhaps because of their worship of the death-loving Great Mother—had the gift of necromancy. With their sorcery, they created trolls: hulking beasts which served them in war. Hiding on a steely peak was what the Ulfr called The Slumbering Beast—a green-scaled dragon—who soon allied with the invading humans and rained fire down upon their cities and temples. The Sorelden were all gone circa 300 Y.E., not to be seen again for five hundred years… until the current Ulfr Crisis (circa 825 Y.E.).

Valkyries: The warrior-maidens who serve Vana and scour Badelgard for worthy additions to the Hall of the Slain. They are portrayed as beautiful, winged women holding spears.

Vana: The goddess of victory and the home. She is portrayed in art as a big-boned, brown-haired woman in a white robe, often plucking her trademark instrument, the harp. She is the original patron goddess of the Badelgard humans; the other deity whom they worship, the Green Dragon, was added to the pantheon after the conquest.

Woodhome: A hunting lodge and general base of operations for the Riverhall Order of Scouts.

White Wolves: A species of Great Wolves with snow-white coats, blue eyes, and viciously territorial tendencies. In winter, they can often be seen rolling in the snow or bounding through the mountains in a never-ending hunt. White Wolf Keep, residence of the Silverback noble family, is named after them.

ABOUT THE AUTHOR

Cursed at birth with a wild imagination, Andrew Cooper spent his youth dreaming of worlds more exciting than Earth.

He is a graduate of the Odyssey Writing Workshop. His stories have appeared in Morpheus Tales, Fear and Trembling, Residential Aliens and Mindflights, among others.

CONTACT THE AUTHOR

Visit **www.aj-cooper.com** to sign up for the newsletter and stay up-to-date on new releases.

Find him on Facebook at:

www.facebook.com/AJCooperauthor